# THE ROWAN MAID

When old Rowan dies, her home in the Welsh mountains is inherited by her son's widow, Mina, and her two children, Cassian and Isobel. Into the valley move Jan Schneider and his mother, Huguenot exiles from the Low Countries. The scene is set for a love affair that goes tragically wrong, for there is evil at Rowan Garth and out of that evil is created Amethyst, the child who should never have been born, twisted branch on a twisted tree.

# THE ROWAN MAID

CATHERINE DARBY

ROBERT HALE · LONDON

© Catherine Darby 1984
First published in Great Britain 1984

ISBN 0 7091 8901 X

Robert Hale Limited
Clerkenwell House
Clerkenwell Green
London EC1R 0HT

Photoset in North Wales by
Derek Doyle & Associates, Mold, Clwyd
Printed and bound in Great Britain by
Garden City Press Limited, Letchworth, Herts.

# *One*

In winter the landscape had a bleak loveliness that transcended the biting wind raging from the heights and the thick mist that crept up from the valleys. The narrow fields were snow-quilted and the pines were black silhouettes against the frozen slate of the cliffs that fell sheer to the valley of Pen Tân. The land was enclosed like a jewel within the cliffs and bordered by a lake, fed by high mountain springs from which a tributary river meandered to the lower valley where Foster Farm was spread out at each side of the broad track that curved past the woollen mill and the rows of cottages where the weavers lived, down to the church, and thence towards the sea.

Amethyst Prester sat her horse and looked down from the high crag that separated the two valleys into the upper vale. The afternoon sunshine was golden on the snow that lay thickly to the very edge of the sparkling water.

In the centre of the white meadows the old house of 'Rowan Garth' stood as it had stood for nearly two hundred years, its slate roof now snow-covered, though in places, the heat of the sun had begun to melt the crisp flakes, the windows glinting in their deep mullions of greystone. The house had been built by an Englishman during the reign of the first Tudor King. Adam Garth had come as a soldier into Wales and fallen in love with the land and with a girl called Rowan who was said to be an illegitimate connection of the king's uncle, Sir Jasper Tudor. Nothing now remained of that time save family tales passed down through the generations, the house that Adam Garth had named for his bride, and the gold serpent ring that twined about Amethyst's finger. She wore it always and constantly glanced at it, her slanting blue eyes having the same intent gleam as the ruby eyes set in the head of the serpent. She would be sixteen at Midsummmer but there were times when her delicate young face, surmounted by a mop of bright red curls, looked much older.

She was thinking now as she gazed down at the house where she had been born how strange it was that people could live their lives and die and be forgotten. She supposed that it would happen to her one day, but she had every intention of living to be very old and of making her mark on the neighbourhood to such an extent that people would find it very difficult to forget. To red hair and eyes of so bright a blue that the very whites seemed tinged with the shade were added a flawless complexion unmarked by the pox and tanned to a pale honey, regular features, a tall slender figure, and a husky voice that sounded always on the edge of a song.

Today she was wearing a riding-habit of slate blue wool with ruffles of white lace at the throat and wrists and a wide brimmed hat with a scarlet feather in the crown. The feather was a protest against Mistress Gerthe's oft-repeated assertion that redheads ought never to wear pink or red,

Amethyst being equally determined to make her own rules. Her pony, Cariad, was her constant companion, indeed her only companion, for Amethyst held aloof from the other younglings in the neighbourhood. Her beginnings had been different from most, for she had been born bastard and her parents had not married until she was nearly fifteen. Now they lived in the house where she had been born and raised and Amethyst lived at Foster Farm which had become her property under the terms of her grandmother's Will.

She remembered Nain Mina only faintly as a faded blonde Englishwoman in a flounced dress that was quite unsuitable for a widow. Nain Mina had borne twin children but the boy, Cassian, had died at twenty and Isobel had borne a bastard child to Jan Schneider, who had managed the mill at Foster Farm. He and his mother had been Huguenots, fleeing from Spanish persecution in the Low Countries when they had come to Wales and settled there. The affair between him and Isobel had ended in some kind of quarrel, the details of which Amethyst had never learned, and Isobel had reared her bastard in proud loneliness until, only the previous year she had informed Amethyst that Jan Schneider was her natural father and that, having made up the old quarrel, they planned at last to marry. The Foster Farm with its mill and weaving-shed now passed to Amethyst and the Pen Tân property would eventually become the possession of Isobel's eldest legitimate child.

It was this child whom Amethyst was now on her way to visit. Born a fortnight before, Harcourt Schneider was the son for whom Jan and Isobel had yearned. He was also the child whose birth made it certain that Amethyst would never be mistress of 'Rowan Garth'.

At that thought her blue eyes glazed to ice over water and her young face bore its ancient look. She slid from Cariad's broad back and began to lead the pony down the steep path that twisted behind the still frozen waterfall to the level ground beneath.

Mounted again she rode towards the house, feeling her heart beat more rapidly. She loved her old home with a passion that she could not diminish though she hid it well. When it had been suggested that she should, upon her parents' marriage, move to Foster Farm and live there with Mistress Gerthe she had smiled sweetly, though inwardly raging, and agreed at once. She had known that her presence would be an embarrassment to the newly wed couple and while she was not in the least concerned with their feelings, the idea of being an unwilling witness to their mutual affection had displeased her.

Jan was salting the yard when she dismounted at the gate and she stood for an instant, her heart in her eyes, watching his broad frame bending to the task, the sunshine drawing the gold out of his light brown hair. She had fallen in love with him before she had learned that he was her father and her only consolation was that she had never betrayed her feelings to anybody. Neither had she succeeded in transmuting them into the affection of a child for a parent. When she saw him her young breasts hardened with desire and there was an odd fluttering in her throat.

"Amethyst!" He straightened up and came over to her, pleasure in his brown eyes. After nearly twenty years in Wales he had scarcely a trace of Flemish accent, though Mistress Gerthe still retained a strong gutteral pronunciation.

"I brought a gift for the baby," Amethyst said smilingly.

"Oh, that was good of you. Is my mother not with you?"
"You know Mistress Gerthe's views on going out in cold weather," Amethyst reminded him.

"She regards it as a Godless practice." He grinned, showing blunt, white teeth, and took Cariad's rein. Amethyst went ahead over the salt-melted snow, pushing ajar the oaken door that led into the great hall. The hall itself rose up to the rafters, its stone walls hung with faded arras, its flagstones covered with sheepskins and goatskins. On the right a door opened into the parlour and a wide staircase led up into a shadowed gallery above.

Amethyst stood for a moment, breathing in the familiar, beloved atmosphere of home. Every stone, every piece of carved dark furniture, every gleaming copper dish was dear to her heart. She had been born and grown up in this house and in her mind no other compared with it. She had always assumed that one day she would be mistress of 'Rowan Garth', and it still seemed incredible that now all this would pass to the new babe.

One of the two servants, Myfi, bustled out from the kitchen, a beaming smile on her elderly face.

"Mistress Amethyst! I didn't expect you today," she exclaimed.

"I decided to come home for an hour," Amethyst said, removing hat and cloak and stamping snow from her boots.

The older woman gave her a glance of sympathy. No doubt it had been sensible for her to be sent to Foster Farm when her mother married but it seemed hard to send the child away from home.

"I shall go up and see my mother," Amethyst said. "She's well?"

"Recovering nicely from her confinement," Myfi answered. "Your little brother is a fine, healthy babe."

Amethyst frowned slightly, not wanting to think of the new babe as her brother.

"I'll go up myself," she said briskly and ran lightly up the staircase and along the gallery. Three small chambers opened off the gallery but Isobel was in the large bedroom over the parlour.

The door was ajar and Isobel was propped up against snowy pillows, a fringed shawl around her shoulders.

Although she was in her late thirties, marriage and motherhood had enhanced the prettiness of her face and soft fair hair drawn back into a froth of ringlets at the nape of her neck. Her large grey eyes lifted from the book in her hands and she gave a faint cool smile with which she masked the embarrassment she felt whenever she saw her daughter.

"How are you, mother?" Amethyst bent to kiss that smooth cheek.

"I feel well enough to get up but the physician insists that I stay here for at least another week," Isobel said.

Jan had not been content to rely on the services of the local midwife but had engaged a physician from Caernarvon to make the difficult journey over the snowbound pass to care for Isobel. It was a measure of his love for his wife, Amethyst supposed, and shook her head slightly as if she were shaking the thought out of existence.

"I brought a gift for the babe," she said stiffly.

"For Harcourt? Oh, how very good of you!" Isobel said enthusiastically.

Her gratitude was a trifle too effusive but she had secretly fretted over Amethyst's reaction to the new babe. It was a relief to find that the girl apparently accepted the situation.

Her daughter had drifted to the foot of the bed, where a beautifully carved wooden cradle held a tightly swaddled bundle. The babe had a fuzz of fine blond hair and his eyes were tightly screwed against the light. Amethyst drew a little silver bell on an ivory stick from the drawstring bag at her waist and shook it playfully.

"Mistress Gerthe brought it with her from the Low Countries," she said. "Jan used it when he was teething."

"Your father," Isobel said.

Amethyst laid the rattle down in the cradle without answering. She would never, in a thousand years, learn to accept Jan Schneider as her father. She had met him only twice before Isobel had confided to her the secret of her birth.

"We meant to marry but there was a foolish quarrel. It was not made up even when you were born. Fourteen years' silence and only a mile between us – so foolish!"

And Amethyst had been expected to accept the situation, to lay aside the cravings that beset her when she looked at Jan and think of him only as her father. She glanced from beneath her lashes and marvelled that her mother could be such a fool.

"The babe looks well," she said, and laid her hand briefly against the round cheek. The ruby-eyed serpent glinted briefly and her eyes were suddenly very blue.

"The physician says that he is healthy but small," Isobel said, and broke off, her face brightening as Jan came in.

"You're not overtiring yourself, my love?" His tone was

solicitous and there was a tenderness in his face as he bent to kiss her.

"Amethyst has brought your old rattle for Harcourt," Isobel said. "Your mother must have kept it all these years!"

"I didn't know," Jan said, smiling across at Amethyst. "He'll be cutting his teeth on it before too long, I dare say."

Amethyst smiled back with closed lips, her lashes still lowered. Her great dread was that by word or look she would betray her feelings to him, but he had eyes only for Isobel. Married eight months, the girl thought in anguish, and already there was a babe in the cradle. They had anticipated their marriage a second time, but this child had been born in wedlock and would, one day, be master of Pen Tân. She hated the newcomer more than she had ever hated anybody in her life and the violence of her own feelings satisfied her in some curious way. She looked down at her brother again, smiling as she said,

"Why is he to be called Harcourt? 'Tis not a family name."

"We wanted a new name, one that had no connection with either of the families," Jan said.

"I expected you to call him Cassian, after your brother who died," Amethyst remarked.

She felt rather than saw the violent start her mother gave, but it was Jan who answered in his calm fashion.

"Your uncle was not a person to be admired, my dear. It is not a good idea to perpetuate his memory."

"Why? What did he do?" Amethyst asked, her curiosity immediately stirred.

"Nothing worth the remembering," Isobel said sharply. "Would you like to hold the baby?" Jan came quickly to the cradle and picked up his son, holding the babe carefully as if he were not accustomed yet to being a father.

"I might drop him," she said sweetly.

Or strangle him or knock his stupid head against the stone wall until his brains fall out.

"I'll give him to your mother, then," Jan said, returning to Isobel's side and laying Harcourt in the crook of her arm. Isobel began to unlace her bodice and bare one round white breast.

Amethyst turned abruptly to the window, staring out over the snow-clad garden. The glimpse she had obtained of her mother's breast had filled her with a shuddering disgust. She could hear Jan whispering as he bent to his wife and child, and Isobel's gurgle of laughter shut the girl out even further from the happy family circle.

"Is my mother truly well?" Jan asked, coming back to where Amethyst stood. "She was not well at Yuletide."

"Oh, it was only a little chill," Amethyst said, moving away slightly lest he put his arm about her. She was certain his hand had just touched her mother's flesh and she had no wish to have him touch her own.

"I will ride over and see her in a day or two," he said. "I have neglected the mill these past weeks."

Although Foster Farm now belonged to Amethyst he had continued to manage it for her. In one way she was glad because it gave her the bitter sweet opportunity to see him nearly every day. In another she longed to be old enough to manage her own affairs so as to be released from the torment of his coming.

"You had more important matters on your mind," Isobel said, not meaning to hurt. She was suckling the baby openly, contentment on her face. Without shame, Amethyst thought, averting her eyes as she bent to kiss her mother's cheek.

"You're not going already!" Jan exclaimed, "You'll stay for supper and I will ride back with you afterwards."

The two of them alone for a while in the crisp, snowly landscape. Amethyst closed her mind against the tempting picture and said brightly,

"Mistress Gerthe will worry if I am not home for supper."

Just as she was unable to call Jan 'father' so she could never bring herself to think of the dumpy little Flemish woman as her grandmother.

"But you'll come again soon?" Isobel said. She had no real desire to see her daughter often. Amethyst had been a difficult child to rear and she had never felt much affection for the girl.

"In a few days." Amethyst took another look at the downy head pressed against the white breast and went out.

"I'll get you some gingerbread," Jan said, following her down the stairs. "Jane made some yesterday."

As if I were a child to be consoled with sweetmeats, Amethyst thought.

"I'm not hungry," she said aloud, "but I'll have a cup of sack before I leave."

"I'll get it." He went past her down the stairs into the parlour.

This wood-panelled chamber ran from front to back of the house and, like the great hall, was warmed by an enormous fire. There were rugs on the floor and embroidered hangings at the windows, and the room had an air of luxury unusual even on a prosperous farm. Amethyst accepted the cup of sack and sat down on the window seat.

"Imagine my mother keeping my rattle for so many years,"

Jan said, pouring wine for himself. "When we fled the Spaniards we had only the clothes we stood up in and whatever we could carry."

"Yes. I know." She sipped her drink, wanting him to go on talking. His deep, slow voice stirred her to the depths of her being.

"He's a fine lad, isn't he?" he said.

"Who? Oh, Harcourt. Yes, a fine lad," she agreed.

"Your mother and I – " Jan hesitated and then went on. "Your mother and I are naturally pleased that we have a son but you mustn't think – you are still our first child."

"But born out of wedlock," she said sweetly.

"Ah, well, we all have things to regret," Jan said awkwardly.

"I shall never regret anything I decide to do," Amethyst said firmly. "I think that one should never regret anything at all."

"But there's no way of avoiding mistakes," he said. Amethyst wondered if she had been one of the mistakes that he now regretted.

"If I ever make a mistake," she said firmly, "I shall ignore it."

"Oh, Amethyst, you're still very young!" he said, laughing.

"You talk as if you were an old man!" she protested. "Why, you're not yet forty."

"And you are not yet sixteen," he returned. "You will learn more sense as you grow older!"

"But my affections will not waver," she said, looking down into the cup. It was the nearest she dare go to confessing her feelings, but he misunderstood as usual, his voice no more than kindly as he said,

"You're a sweet child. Shall I ride down with you to Foster Farm?"

"My mother will fret about you if you go riding on the ice," Amethyst said.

"Aye, she worries if I'm long absent from her side," he said.

There was a touch of complacency in his voice that amused and irritated her. She wondered how long her mother's possessiveness would continue to delight him and when he would grow weary of her clinging ways.

"And Mistress Gerthe will fret if I'm long away," she said lightly, putting down the cup and rising. "I'll get my outdoor garments from the kitchen and have a word with Myfi and Jane. Will you bring Cariad round to the front, Jan?"

"Your servant, Mistress Amethyst." He made a leg and grinned at her as she went out. She had accepted the marriage with good grace, he thought, but there was a constraint between them for all that. He could feel it most strongly when they were alone together, and he had no idea how to overcome it. It was likely, despite his and Isobel's efforts, that the girl felt jealous of the new babe but that would be remedied when Amethyst found a young man of her own. A frown creased his brow and the shadow of an old trouble darkened his eyes. He put down his own cup and went through to the hall.

He was not yet accustomed to being master of 'Rowan Garth'. His boyhood had been spent in a modest Flemish house and for more than ten years he had occupied the small whitewashed farmstead of the Foster property. In less

than a year he had won back the sweetheart he had lost years
before, sired a male heir, and found himself owner of a
prosperous farm. It had all happened too quickly for his
slow and careful nature to absorb, and he still found himself
waking in the handsome bedchamber with a sense of shock.

Amethyst had donned her hat and cloak again, but
lingered to speak to Myfi.

"There is sickness over at the Bohanna house," the old
servant was informing her. "Sore throats and chills. You'd
best keep away."

"Mistress Gerthe told me. She ventured there herself a
few days since."

The Bohannas had been stewards at Pen Tân for years.
Old Daniel Bohanna had died a few months before and his
son Will now headed a family of young unmarried sisters.

"Is she sick too?" Myfi asked.

"A cold, nothing more. Mistress Gerthe will live for
ever," Amethyst said with a touch of gloom.

"Not unkind to you, is she?" the servant asked.

"No, she is very good," Amethyst said with a slight
grimace.

Jan's mother did her best to make the girl feel
comfortable and at ease in Foster Farm, but she made it
clear that in her opinion Amethyst had been badly reared.
In Mistress Gerthe's world young ladies did not ride about
the countryside by themselves but stayed demurely at home,
cooking and sewing and waiting for a young man to come
courting. Amethyst disliked domestic tasks and had every
intention of finding her own husband when the time came.
He would be a healthy and prosperous gentleman, she had
decided, and would always allow her to have her own way.

There was no room for romantic yearnings in her plans, for she was quite certain that she would never fall in love with anybody. Jan had too strong a hold on her heart and since he was forbidden to her she had laid aside any notions of love.

He was calling to her now from the front yard and she gave Myfi a swift hug and went out to where he held Cariad's rein.

"Will you come over to the mill soon?" she asked wistfully as she mounted.

"In a few days." He took her hand briefly and stepped back. "Give my love to my mother. I hope her cold is not too severe."

"Not in the least." Amethyst smiled and slapped Cariad lightly on the rump. She didn't look back, knowing that he would have already gone back to his wife and son.

She rode back slowly, Cariad's hoofs crunching the deep snow. The sky looked as if it had been newly washed and the lake sparkled, but her heart was heavy. The babe was healthy. Though her mother was near forty she had borne a healthy boy and no doubt there would be more to follow. She guessed that her father, after so many years of restraint, was eager to prove his manhood as often as possible. The thought hurt almost unbearably but she dwelt on it, turning it over in her mind, probing it like an aching tooth.

At the waterfall she dismounted and scrambled up the icy path to the top of the crag from whence the track wound more gently down to the lower valley. The Foster land had been brought into the family nearly a century before when a young woman called Abigail Foster had married the master of 'Rowan Garth'. It had been a modest sheep-farm then.

Later on it had been used as a stud farm for the sturdy Welsh cobs that carried farmers to and from the market-place. Since Jan Schneider had come to Wales the property had been developed as a woollen mill, fine cloth being spun from the fleeces of the Pen Tân flocks and sold along the borders. At the other side of the track the mill with its long weaving-shed and the counting-house rose at the side of the river. Nearly a hundred men, most of them trained by Jan himself, were employed here and lived in the cottages farther down the vale. Jan, though he still managed the mill, took no payment for the long hours he put in, and the profits were being saved.

"To provide you with a secure future, my dear," Isobel had said.

And as compensation because she would now never own Pen Tân, Amethyst thought, her lip curling slightly as she mounted again and rode towards the small, whitewashed house where she had lived since her mother's marriage. It might be good enough for Mistress Gerthe, she thought, but not for Amethyst Prester. There were only four rooms, comfortably furnished and kept in a state of sparkling cleanliness by the little Flemish woman, but they had none of the timeless elegance of the chambers at 'Rowan Garth'.

The girl dismounted at the gate and called to the stable-lad to take Cariad. As she pushed open the front door into the narrow passage she heard Mistress Gerthe's voice raised in admonishment.

"Scrape the snow from your boots!"

Amethyst obeyed, scowling, and went past the tiny parlour into the big cheerful kitchen where Mistress Gerthe was brewing a tisane at the fire.

"Hang your cloak to dry and take off your boots, child. Would you like a hot drink?" she enquired, turning her neatly coiled white head.

"Shall I make it?" Amethyst draped her cloak over one of the two high-backed chairs set at each side of the hearth and sat down to tug off her boots.

"My chill is almost gone," Mistress Gerthe said. "I dosed myself with honey and coltsfoot. The Bohannas ought to take it. I hear Susan Bohanna is worse."

"The babe is well," Amethyst said, leaning her head down to the heat of the fire. The flames were like mirror images of her tangled curls and the firelight cast scarlet shadows over her long, slim unchildlike hands.

"The little dear!" Mistress Gerthe's round pink face creased into a fond smile as she poured the steaming beverage into a copper mug. "My first grandson! Mark my words, there'll be more to follow."

'I was your first granddaughter,' the girl thought, 'but I went through my childhood without your affection for fourteen years. I lived a mile away from you and not once, by word or look, did you ever seek to know me. So you may keep your kind smiles now. I want no part of them.'

"You ought to take care when you go riding in this weather," the other was continuing, seating herself opposite. "Your pony might easily break a leg on the ice."

"I was anxious to see my baby brother again," Amethyst said sweetly.

"I hoped they might choose a Flemish name," Mistress Gerthe said, "but your mother wanted an English name that sounded grand and rich."

"My grandmother named me," Amethyst said. "When I

was born she said my eyes were blue as amethysts and so named me."

"Mistress Mina was a flightly woman," the other said, pursing her mouth.

"She was very kind to me," Amethyst said.

"Well I'm sure she was very fond of you," Mistress Gerthe allowed. "Was your mother well?"

"Quite well." Amethyst spoke with deliberate indifference, knowing that the other wanted to talk about Jan but taking a perverse pleasure in denying her.

"I shall go up and see the baby in a few days," Mistress Gerthe said. "The snow will begin to melt soon, now that the milder weather is coming."

Amethyst left her to chatter on in her boring amiable fashion and went out of the kitchen and up the stairs to the larger of the two bedrooms. The chamber in which she had slept since coming to Foster Farm was a pleasant apartment with a yellow coverlet over the wide bed matching the curtains at the window. There was rush matting laid over the floor and blue bowls with bulbs in them on the windowsill. It had a charm of its own but she had not yet learned to feel at home in it. She had in fact not troubled to try.

In the corner of the room was a carved prayer-stool which she had brought with her from 'Rowan Garth'. Amethyst had never been one for praying overlong. The stool had belonged to a Catholic forbear and, aware of the Huguenot dislike of popery, the girl took a sly delight on kneeling on it in an attitude of deep devotion when Mistress Gerthe looked in to say goodnight.

Now, however, she knelt upon the stool with sincerity throbbing in every whispered word.

"Dear Lord! let the babe die quickly! Make me mistress of 'Rowan Garth'. Let the babe die, God. Let it catch cold and shiver into a fever and die. I'll not regret it. I swear by the blood in my veins and the serpent on my hand that I will regret nothing."

It was a good, strong prayer, she decided. She would go on repeating it for a while until she was quite certain that Heaven had heard.

## Two

"He was so little," Jan said, his features contorting into a grimace of pain. "Such a little thing but the physician thought him healthy. My mother said he didn't look well when she visited but we thought it only a little cold. It is hard for Isobel."

"And for you," Amethyst said quickly. She didn't want to talk about her mother's grief, but she did want to comfort Jan, to hold him tightly against her and make him forget his sorrow.

"Harcourt Schneider," he said slowly, as if he were committing the name to memory. "At least he was baptised – and there will be other babes."

"Oh, no!" The exclamation slipped out of her before it could be checked.

"What?" He turned to give her a puzzled frowning glance.

"My mother isn't a young woman," Amethyst said hastily.

"She's not yet eight and thirty," he said, smiling slightly. "I suppose that seems very ancient to your age but she is capable of bearing many more children to ease our loss."

"Yes, of course."

She wanted to scream out that he and Isobel already had a child born fifteen years before their marriage, but she kept her voice low and sweet. Perhaps she ought not to blame Jan for his lack of fatherly feeling. She, for her own part, had the greatest difficulty in thinking of him as her parent.

Spring hesitated on the horizon. They were walking in the field by the weaving-shed and the snow was melting fast into puddles, spears of new grass rising into the pale sunlight. He had come down as usual, to look over the work, to check on the looms and talk to the men, most of whom paused to mutter their condolences. Amethyst went too, not because she was interested in the spinning and weaving of wool but because it was her opportunity to be with him, free from the presence of either Isobel or Mistress Gerthe.

"The Bohanna girls are better," she said more cheerfully.

"But two other babes died lower down the valley." His own voice was sad and reflective.

"Mistress Gerthe says that some diseases attack adults lightly but are fatal for the young," she said gravely.

"My mother is fond of the young," he said. "She went down to do what she could for the families but even her skill was of no avail."

"I know." She nodded and patted his arm in a consoling little gesture, her face gentle. For a moment she sensed, rather than felt, his sudden withdrawal and then he smiled at her and said.

"We must put aside gloomy thoughts. When are you coming to 'Rowan Garth'? Your mother will be glad of your company."

Isobel had not the faintest desire to spend time with her daughter, Amethyst knew, but she said at once, "Oh, I shall come up in a few days when she is feeling a little better."

"Good girl." He spoke in the tone that put her firmly back into childhood again and the brief, disturbing, curiously intimate moment was gone.

Amethyst quickened her step slightly as they turned back towards the house.

"Will you stay for a meal?" she began but he shook his head, leaving her behind as he crossed the track and called out to his mother, who had just emerged into the yard. They stood together speaking in Flemish, the language that excluded Amethyst. The girl approached them slowly, dragging her feet a little. She hated seeing Jan with his mother almost as much as she hated seeing him with Isobel. The dumpy little woman in the neat black dress had a bond with him that Amethyst had never had with anybody. She had never enjoyed an uncomplicated affection for anyone.

"Come and change your boots, child," Mistress Gerthe broke off to say. "We cannot have you being ill too."

Her voice was scolding as it frequently was when she addressed Amethyst. The truth was that she never felt at ease with the girl though she had readily agreed to chaperon her at Foster Farm. She had lost two baby girls before Jan's birth and, dearly as she loved her son, she had always yearned for a daughter. But Mistress Gerthe's imagined damsel was not in the least like the tall, sly-eyed girl who lived with her at Foster Farm. Amethyst was invariably obedient and gentle but there was something about her that made the older woman uneasy.

"If I am, you will have to give me one of your remedies," she said.

"Ah! they did the other babes no good," Mistress Gerthe said sadly.

Amethyst gave Jan a swift dismissing nod and went into the house, scraping the soles of her boots noisily as she entered the hall. The curtains were still partly drawn in token of mourning and the crackling of flames in the hearth was an intrusion upon the quiet. Amethyst went into the kitchen and stood, looking down into the bright fire. It was unfortunate that an answered prayer had to mean unhappiness for the only person she loved but Jan deserved a little punishment for loving her mother so much, and Harcourt had not been on earth long enough for his going to leave much of a gap. She tightened her lips as she heard Mistress Gerthe's voice.

"Poor Jan bears his loss very bravely. We must pray there are other children."

'To inherit Pen Tân which would have come to me if my parents had married before my birth,' the girl thought, but she remained silent, her eyes on the fire.

"So cruel to lose a babe," Mistress Gerthe was continuing. "I know what it means, my dear. I hope you never will. You must go often to see your mother. This is a sad time for us all. I am only thankful that my remedies have proved more successful for the Bohannas. Susan is a lot better, they tell me."

"I think I will saddle Cariad and ride down to the church," Amethyst said abruptly.

"To church, my dear?" Mistress Gerthe looked slightly surprised, Amethyst not being noted for her piety.

"For a little while. I feel the need of it," Amethyst murmured.

Mounted on Cariad she rode through the melting snow, past the mill and the long weaving-sheds, towards the grey church huddled like an old woman against the hill and the yew trees standing guard over the slanting tombstones. The graves of many of those who had owned or lived at Pen Tân were scattered there, the older ones moss-grown and with Latin inscriptions, belonging as they did to a vanished Catholic age, the newer ones less florid. Amethyst could read no Latin but she glanced at the varying names when she had tethered Cariad to the gate and was strolling down the path. 'Rowan Price, dead in 1584 at the age of ninety-four'. She had been daughter to the first Rowan for whom the house had been built. Her great grandson, Caleb Prester, had died in the same year and been laid next to her and, on his other side, was his wife, Abigail, who had brought the Foster property into the family.

'My great-great-grandmother,' Amethyst thought, staring at the carved angel that stood guard over the grave.

Farther along, Rowan Prester and Jasper Prester were buried side by side, though they had been brother and sister-in-law, not wed.

"It was a sad scandal," Isobel had told her once. "Rowan was cousin to Thomas and Jasper Prester. She wed Tom and bore your grandfather Walter, but after Tom's death she took Jasper for her lover and Walter killed them both."

He had been hanged for his crime, and his widow, Mina, had borne twins and reared them alone, only to have Cassian die at twenty and Isobel bear a bastard daughter to the man she would marry fifteen years later.

Cassian's grave was apart from the others, set in rough ground behind a hedge of yew, Amethyst had once wondered why, but Isobel had said vaguely there was no particular reason for it.

The latest recruit to the ranks of the dead had been buried with his grandmother, Mina, and his name added to the stone, the chisel marks still raw in the slate.

'Harcourt Schneider. Born 1673'. There was a stone jar with some trails of holly in it. Amethyst knelt and moved the jar so that the sprays of red-berried green obliterated the name. Now Harcourt was gone as if he had never been and her full lips curved into a gently reflective smile.

"Good morrow, Mistress Amethyst." A footfall behind her and a pleasant masculine voice brought her to her feet. Will Bohanna stood there, a bunch of snowdrops in his hand, shy pleasure on his face. At eighteen he was a handsome, well-set youth with curly black hair and an air of gentleness that contrasted with his rough working clothes.

"Good morrow." She gave him a smile suitable for the place in which they stood and the black habit which she wore.

"I brought some flowers for the Evans babes," he said, indicating the snowdrops. "Their mam is too grieved to set foot out of doors."

"That was kind of you. Mistress Gerthe told me they had died despite all she had tried to do."

"Ah, she did her best," he allowed, "and my sisters are both better. Susan is a mite shaky yet but that will pass. Better than the apothecary is Mistress Gerthe for all that she's a foreigner."

The Flemish woman would always be regarded as a foreigner, Amethyst thought. She was pleased, feeling herself to be a part of the fabric of life in the high valleys with no fear that she would ever be regarded as a stranger. She looked with newly awakened interest at the curly-headed young man. Will Bohanna was only the steward and his five sisters would all require dowries, but he was healthy and handsome and not likely ever to leave the district. She would be sixteen soon and she might as well marry somebody.

"I'll walk with you to the Evans grave," she offered, suiting action to words and allowing the tips of her fingers to rest on his arm as they strolled along the path to where a pathetic mound, as yet unmarked by slate, signified the last resting-place of the Evans children.

"Thank you, mistress." Will looked slightly surprised at her unwonted friendliness, and she murmured demurely, "Amethyst, if you please. I would like to have you call me Amethyst."

"Amethyst, then." He had flushed but his long lashed grey eyes were admiring.

She lifted her own vividly blue ones to his face and heard herself say, "I like to hear you call me so. Most people call me mistress, except for Mistress Gerthe and she calls me 'child'."

"Surely your mother calls you by your name!"

"My mother prefers to speak to me as seldom as possible," Amethyst said sadly. "One cannot blame her for I am a constant reminder of her past folly, and now that she is respectably wed – "

"One could never hold your birth against you," Will said fervently.

"The world," said Amethyst vaguely, "can be exceedingly cruel. Shall I put the flowers on the earth for you? If we stick them in the soil they will look as if they are still growing."

He handed her the snowdrops and she knelt, patting them

into place with a narrow hand. The sunlight struck fire from
the red curls clustered at the nape of her neck and Will bent,
pulling one to its full length and letting it spring back.

"Why did you do that?" She had risen and stood close to
him, her breath soft on his face.

"Because you're most lovely," he said on a breathless
note.

"Kiss me then," she said softly.

"Mis – Amethyst, 'tis bad fortune to kiss in a graveyard,"
Will stammered, but she laughed softly, winding her arms
about his neck, her mouth open against his own.

He had kissed girls before but never one so vibrant,
clinging to him as if she lacked strength of her own. Her lips
were warm and soft, drawing desire from him. His hands
circled her narrow waist and he could feel the hard promise
of her young breasts under the velvet of her bodice.

"We must make our own luck, Will," she said huskily, "I
always do."

"Your lady mother would be angered," he gasped out.
"She thinks me over-young to fill my father's shoes as it is
and she'll not approve of my dallying with her daughter."

"My mother ᴠ ed her mill manager, so she's small room
to talk," Amethyst said scornfully.

Will, whose mind was not yet running on weddings, gave
a slight start.

"Wouldn't you like to walk out with me?" Amethyst
enquired. "Wouldn't you?"

"I never thought about it," he said frankly.

"Think about it." She slipped from his grasp and stood,
slim as a wand, her eyes laughing. "Come, we'll walk back
together. You'd like to escort me home, wouldn't you?"

Bewildered and delighted, he nodded and she slipped her hand through his arm and went with him to where Cariad was tethered, looping the reins over her arm.

"Can you read, Will?" she enquired as they made their way out on to the track again.

"Of course I can read!" He sounded slightly indignant.

"Then I can lend you some books," she offered. "I have some poems. Do you like poems, Will?"

"I never read any," he said flatly.

"Oh, well, never mind." She shrugged elegantly. Perhaps it had been too much to hope that her future husband would be as well educated as he was handsome.

"I like to sing," he said shyly, "and I know a deal about birds and foxes and suchlike. We could go riding together if you've a mind. I know many hidden places where the flowers bloom after the snows are come."

There was one such place she knew about herself. She had met Jan Schneider there and talked with him, not knowing then that he was her father.

"Will you be in church on Sunday?" she changed the conversation to ask.

"I always am."

"Then you may ride home with me. Where's your horse today?"

"Still tied up at the back of the church," he said blankly. "You put all else out of my head!"

"Oh, Will!" She paused, leaning with her head against his broad shoulder in a consciously kittenish gesture. "You must keep your mind on what you are doing else folk will begin to suspect."

"There's nothing to suspect," he said in his literal way.

"That we are walking out together. You have not altered your mind in the space of a few minutes, have you?"

"It's only that I usually ride home from church with Heulwen Evans," he said, looking acutely embarrassed. "It is not a spoken arrangement. It just falls out that way most Sabbaths."

Heulwen was small and pretty with soft, thin brown hair and a thin mouth. Later in life she would grow shrill and nagging but youth lent her charm. Amethyst said carefully.

"Have you made any promise to her?"

"No. We are in the way of friendship."

"Then she cannot complain if you ride home from church with me," Amethyst said. "But we'll wait a week or two. She will be needing the comfort of a friend when she lost her two little sisters so recently."

He had not expected such tactful sympathy from her, Amethyst Prester had always struck him as a rather cool and haughty piece who never mingled with the other younglings in the district. Her ardour had taken him completely by surprise, for she had never done more than greet him briefly, and the prospect of walking out with her was breathtaking. He was not even certain if he wanted to marry anybody yet. At eighteen, with a widowed mother and five unmarried sisters, he felt the weight of his responsibilities.

"Dear Will!" Amethyst said, blue eyes glinting at him through thick lashes tipped with sunlight. Her skin had the same golden tinge and her mouth was pink, the lower lip full and sensual.

Greatly daring, he kissed her again and she pressed herself against him, the slim length of her throbbing and quivering. The white house was in view, the long sheds, the walled paddock where horses had once been bred before the mill was built. She spun away from him and said, her voice coaxing,

"All this is mine, Will. My grandmother left it to me. The man I choose to marry will be master of all this."

"I have a house of my own," he said, his pride flicked by some quality in her voice that jarred on him. "And my post as steward is well paid, very well paid indeed."

"Of course it is, but a man loses nothing by seeking to advance himself," she said.

"I'd not wish to offend or to hurt poor Heulwen."

"Then you have made promise!"

"No, I haven't, but perhaps something is understood – expected from our two families," he said awkwardly.

"Then I'll not intrude," she said, her voice small and hurt.

"It isn't that. Give me a little time," he said quickly. "When Heulwen is out of mourning and in less need of comfort, then it will not seem so unkind to abandon her little by little. I swear there have been no promises between us."

"Thank you, Will." She smiled at him and turned to lead Cariad into the narrower walk that led to the stables. He stayed where he was, staring after her, excitement and apprehension stirring in him. He was not a young man given to analysing his own feelings, but now he began to wonder if he had been in love with Amethyst Prester and not known it for a long time.

"You were talking to Master Bohanna," Mistress Gerthe observed, coming down the narrow staircase.

"Were you spying on me?" Amethyst asked sharply.

"I was in the bedroom," the older woman said with dignity. "I saw you kiss him, child. That was not well done. Maids should have modesty."

"I shall kiss whom I please," Amethyst said haughtily, sweeping into the parlour.

It was a chilly little room, sparsely furnished with, despite the fire, none of the comfort of the parlour at 'Rowan Garth'.

"But in public, when you are still in mourning for the babe – "

"There was nobody to see us except you, and you should not have been looking," Amethyst said crossly.

"I happened to look out through the window. It is possible that others may have done the same. There were men in the weaving-sheds. But even if you had been entirely alone it was not good to kiss so shamelessly. And Master Bohanna is a steward for your mother's estate! She would not be pleased to hear of such wanton behaviour."

"And no doubt you will inform her," Amethyst said.

"I will say nothing," Mistress Gerthe said. "I must have your promise that such a thing will not happen again. It would reflect very badly on me, for I am your chaperon and you are in my care. I am responsible for you, child, and I will rear you as I would rear my own daughter."

"I am near sixteen and already reared," the girl said.

"Perhaps you think so." Mistress Gerthe smiled slightly in a manner that intensely irritated the younger girl. "I remember feeling very grown up when I was only fifteen too, but it is not so. While I am here you are in my care and you will do as you are told. I shall require a solemn promise from you that you will not behave in such a manner again, else I will be forced to speak to your mother."

"Perhaps I want to marry him," Amethyst argued.

"Ah, marriage is a fine thing," Mistress Gerthe said, "but you are too young and untried to choose a husband yet. Marriage is a serious matter to be discussed between two people and their families. It is not a matter of kissing in a meadow. And this is the first I have heard of you wanting to wed anybody. I did not know that you and Master Bohanna were even friends."

"We are not," the girl said quickly. "I was jesting with him, that's all."

"Not a kindly jest." The other pursed her lips in disapproval. "Now you must give me your word that you will do no such thing again. I cannot countenance such behaviour."

"I promise," Amethyst said, becoming sweetly meek again, her brief flare of rebellion apparently dying.

"You give me your word, your solemn word?"

"My word of honour." The blue eyes were guileless. "I have behaved very foolishly, Mistress Gerthe. It was the impulse of a moment, no more."

"Such impulses should be controlled," the other said.

"I am very sorry for it," Amethyst said. "Truly such conduct will not happen again."

"Then we will say no more. Go up and change your boots. You are dirtying my clean floors." Mistress Gerthe said.

'My floors,' Amethyst thought. 'This is my property and you are here to keep house for me, though you choose to forget it'.

Aloud she said gently, "And you take such trouble over them too. You work so hard though we could easily afford a servant."

"I never met a servant yet who could clean and cook as well as I do," Mistress Gerthe said.

"And to help the neighbours as you do."

"It is our duty to try to help our neighbours. Our Christian duty."

"Will was telling me that the Evans family are in sad case," Amethyst remarked, sitting on the stairs to tug at her boots.

"They lost two babes in the recent sickness," the other nodded.

"And poor Heulwen is delicate. She has a weak chest, Will says."

"I will brew an infusion and take it to her," Mistress Gerthe said promptly.

"And I will change my shoes," Amethyst said, springing up lightly and giving the other a gentle smile. "You are not cross with me now, are you?"

"The young are often foolish," Mistress Gerthe said tolerantly.

Privately she considered the girl had inherited the wanton blood of her mother and needed discipline. Perhaps it might not be bad if Will Bohanna did eventually marry her. He was a sensible young man who was carrying out his work as a steward in a manner that Jan considered exemplary. But kissing him in public was definitely to be discouraged.

Amethyst put on a thinner pair of shoes and hung up her cloak. From her window it was perfectly possible to look out across the melting snow to where she had paused to embrace Will. Goddam Mistress Gerthe and her prying! The old woman was always where she was least wanted. Talking Flemish with Jan. Speaking of Foster Farm as if it were her own property. For ever lecturing and scolding.

Amethyst went downstairs again, took a winter apple from a box of them in the kitchen, and made her way along the covered passage to the stables. Once there had been twenty mares and stallions here. Now there were only Cariad and Mistress Gerthe's piebald.

The stable-lad was perched on a stool, polishing brasses. Amethyst greeted him in Welsh, gave Cariad the apple and wandered back to the lad, dropping down to the straw beside him.

"I am in disgrace," she observed, taking one of the brasses and squinting at it critically.

"Oh?" The boy gave her a puzzled glance.

"For mingling with my inferiors," Amethyst said. "Mistress Gerthe complains that I spend too much time talking to Will Bohanna and to Heulwen Evans. She will not countenance my going to the Evans house even, to pay my condolences to Mistress Evans."

"She fears the infection for you," the lad suggested.

"The infection is spent." Amethyst rose impatiently, throwing down the brass and shaking out her skirts. "It is only that Mistress Gerthe doesn't wish me to make any friends. She is a jealous old besom!"

The stable-lad was watching her with lively curiosity. He was not used to his young mistress imparting any confidences to him and he had no idea what she wanted him to say in return. For lack of inspiration he grunted and went on with his polishing.

"She will have to learn that I make what friends I please," Amethyst said. "If I obey her dictates I will be left with only Cariad for company."

She swung away and went back into the house, leaving the

boy to stare after her. He was a stupid boy, she thought, but he was also a gossip. She had seen him chattering and whispering with some of the local lads.

"Oh, you should not have gone out to the stables in your slippers," Mistress Gerthe said, turning from the fire, where she was boiling water.

"It's dry there."

"But there is straw on your skirt. That will need to be sponged and brushed now! Really, child, you go about to make a nuisance of yourself!"

"I'll help you now that I'm here," Amethyst said. "What do you want me to do?"

"Stir this and don't let it boil over. I am infusing some rosemary and honey for a sleeping draught. Mistress Evans needs some sound sleep if she is to recover from her bereavement."

"It is Heulwen who has the weak chest, though Will tells me she will not admit to it," Amethyst said, taking the wooden spoon and bending over the bubbling mixture.

"I have a jar of coltsfoot and honey in the pantry. I'll take it to her when I go to see Mistress Evans."

"I'll get it for you." Amethyst left her stirring and went into the narrow pantry with its shelves of neatly labelled jars. Dill, cumin, aniseed, caraway, wild garlic, rosemary, thyme – the list seemed endless. On a higher shelf less innocent herbs used in the tiniest quantity for specific ailments, were ranged. Pennyroyal for cramping period pains, foxglove to quicken a sluggish heart, asafoetida for teething fits, poppy to relieve pain. Mistress Gerthe grew and gathered most of the herbs herself, pounding ointments, brewing infusions and tisanes.

"What on earth are you doing in there?" Mistress Gerthe demanded, hurrying to rescue the boiling pot from calamity.

"Looking for the coltsfoot physic," Amethyst's voice floated back.

"Second shelf on the right. You cannot miss it."

"I have it." Amethyst emerged, the squat bottle in her hand.

"I will leave this to cool and then take them both over to the Evans' house – unless you wish to save me the ride." Mistress Gerthe spoke hopefully, being less than enthusiastic about going out into the cold.

"I have to clean my skirt before the stains eat into it," Amethyst said.

"Go and do it now, then. We'll eat supper when I return from Mistress Evans."

"I'll make it ready." The girl set down the bottle of dark fluid and went serenely out.

Mistress Gerthe put the pot of boiling rosemary aside to cool and began to take off the large white apron which she habitually wore over her black gown. Amethyst being helpful was nearly as much trouble as Amethyst being difficult, she thought wryly. Perhaps, after all, it was too late and she was too old to bring up a young girl in the way that she should go.

In her bedroom with the yellow counterpane over the bed, Amethyst knelt at her prayer-stool. For a few moments she knelt motionless, her long fingers folded into a flame, her blue eyes closed. Then she raised her head and began to tell God what she had decided.

# Three

"It was not the sickness that killed her," Will said. "The physician told her mam that the sickness killed only the very young or the very old."

"Heulwen was always delicate," Amethyst said. "Perhaps the infection stayed in her bones or something."

"The infection has run its course," Will objected. "And Heulwen died so quickly. She had a little fever and then sank into a deep sleep and never woke up. The physician said he had never seen anything like it before."

"You are not suggesting she was poisoned, are you?" Amethyst said lightly.

"Poisoned? The idea never came into my head!" he exclaimed.

"Of course not. It's a foolish idea," she said quickly and reassuringly. "Poor Mistress Gerthe would be terribly upset if she thought her physic had caused – "

"Caused what?"

"Heulwen's two baby sisters died and my own little brother too. Mistress Gerthe was quite certain that her medicines were much better than the physician's, but she is getting old and forgetful."

"But surely she is not so old? She cannot be more than sixty!"

"Let us hope it is forgetfulness," Amethyst murmured. "Oh, Will, I was so sorry to hear about Heulwen! I was truly sorry about that. I know she was a friend of yours."

"Not such a good friend," he objected.

"You walk home with her from church. Mistress Gerthe said – "

"What did Mistress Gerthe say?" Will asked sharply.

"Oh, she saw us kissing in the meadow," Amethyst said. "She was very angry about it. She told me that you spent your time with Heulwen Evans and that Heulwen was bent on marrying you."

"But I told you myself that we were friendly," he protested.

"I told Mistress Gerthe that but she said we were a pair of innocents and that Heulwen would get you in the end. She feared I might be hurt, you see."

Will Bohanna shook his head slightly. He was completely bewildered by the turn of events, and her talk confused him. A few days ago he had been plain Will Bohanna, steward at Pen Tân, with more responsibilities than most young men of his age and a vague understanding with Heulwen Evans which might blossom into something more. Now he was walking out with Amethyst Prester and, without quite knowing how it had come about, and he was looking forward to being master of Foster Farm, and Heulwen was dead. Suddenly dead after Mistress Gerthe's physic.

"One gets such foolish notions when one is too much alone," Amethyst was saying. "Mistress Gerthe is so very fond of me, so very anxious that I should never be hurt or not obtain whatever I want. She is a most determined woman."

"You just said she was forgetful," he reminded her.

"Oh, I hope so. I do hope it is forgetfulness," she said earnestly. "It would be terrible if it were anything else."

"What else could it be?" he demanded.

"Nothing. Nothing at all, and you must not put suspicions into my head," she said. "Come! I'll race you to the top of the slope!"

She had ridden out to where he had been ploughing a steep furrow and persuaded him into taking a walk with her. Today she had put off her mourning dress in favour of a blue habit and a hat with lace sewed in clusters inside the brim. The March wind was blustering and her skirts whipped up around her slender ankles as she ran. As a child she had worn tunics and breeches, he recalled, but now she was all femininity, her red ringlets bobbing at the nape of her neck, her blue eyes shaming the sky.

He was a moment behind her at the crest of the field and she turned, holding out her hands to pull him up the steep slope, her mouth open against his own.

"Someone may see!" he gasped out.

"Who's to see?" She let him go and sat down on the grass. "And if they do – we're free people."

"And I'm your mam's steward."

"And my mother married her mill manager. It runs in the family!"

"But they had you," Will said.

"Ah! it is all right to beget a child on a woman and marry her fifteen years later, is it?" Amethyst exclaimed.

"Will you do that, Will? Beget a bastard on me and then

wed me after fifteen years have passed?"

"I'll never touch you save in honour," he protested.

"But there's no harm in kissing," Amethyst argued.

"I know, but – "

"Or is it that you don't like kissing me? Is that it? Did you like kissing Heulwen Evans more?"

"No, of course not."

"Then you did kiss her!"

"Once or twice. It was nothing serious."

"I knew she wanted to wed you," Amethyst said in triumph. "I told Mistress Gerthe it wasn't so but she was quite certain. She swore you were merely trifling with my affections and she was very sorry for me because she didn't want me to be hurt."

"I never trifled with anything," Will said helplessly. "It was you who first came to me!"

"I knew you would cast that up at me sooner or later," Amethyst said sadly.

"I cast nothing up, but you have me in such a muddle I cannot tell which end is up! You twist words around and make them mean something else! I cannot tell where or what the meaning is any longer!"

"I want us to be married," she said gently, looking up at him from where she sat. "It is too soon yet to announce our betrothal, but I will be sixteen at Midsummer and you may speak to my mother then. She will not raise objections. She will be pleased that I have chosen such a fine young man, I promise you!"

"I am still in confusion," Will began, and her temper snapped at the lack of comprehension in his face.

"Then go and plough your furrow and get your confusion

sorted!" she said rudely. "Or weep at Heulwen's grave if you choose! Lord, but I begin to think she was welcome to you!"

"Fine! I'm neglecting my work as it is!" he flung back, and strode off down the hill again.

He was really quite stupid, she thought, leaning back and tipping her hat over her eyes. And he had been fonder of Heulwen Evans than he had admitted. It was most convenient that the wench had died. She would have been a barrier, a tugging at Will's heartstrings, a shadow of guilt in his slow, honest mind.

There remained Mistress Gerthe. Amethyst had two courses of action open to her and was still not certain which one to pursue. She could so work upon the minds of those around her that Mistress Gerthe would be regarded as criminally foolish or even a poisoner. The choice was hers to make and her own uncertainty was delicious. She smiled, lips curving, and felt rather than heard Will Bohanna come tramping back to her.

"We ought not to quarrel," he began, twisting his hat round and round in his hands.

"I am not quarrelling," Amethyst returned, not opening her eyes or shifting her position.

"The truth is that I need time," he said unhappily. "It never entered my head that you and I would ever – it takes time to grow accustomed to change."

"I said we would make no announcement yet," Amethyst said, opening her eyes a slit.

"And you are not angry? I truly had no deep affection for Heulwen."

"Lord, I never thought you had," Amethyst said. "It was

Mistress Gerthe put that into my head. Go and do your ploughing! I will see you another day."

He hesitated, bent down and kissed her swiftly on the cheek and was gone before she could object or reason. He would be an easy husband to manage, she thought, raising her head to watch him hurry back to his plough. He was handsome too. She could not have borne a plain husband.

'And I must marry someone,' she thought as she had thought many times before. With the man she loved forbidden to her she was determined not to spend her life alone, and Will Bohanna was better than most. She sighed and sat up, brushing grass from her clothes, watching his figure recede into the distance. She could be as rude as she pleased and he would always be the one who came back to apologise. The knowledge gave her a dreary satisfaction.

After Heulwen there were no more deaths, but she sensed a change in the attitude of the villagers towards Mistress Gerthe. There was nothing definite upon which she could put her finger, only a few sidelong glances, the faintest withdrawal when Mistress Gerthe came out of church on a Sunday. Amethyst herself said nothing but she knew that the other was puzzled and slightly hurt.

"For it seems that once a fever has run its course one's services are no longer required," she said a trifle bitterly.

"You don't want the sickness to come again just so you can dole out your physic, do you?" Amethyst asked.

"Of course not, foolish child. I simply meant that one likes to be useful. But nobody has asked me for a remedy since."

"Since Heulwen Evans died," Amethyst murmured. They were in the kitchen together, laying the table for supper.

"What is that supposed to mean?" Mistress Gerthe frowned.

"Nothing, but Heulwen Evans did die and she wasn't even very sick."

"The fever must have run to her lungs and killed her. I've known such a thing happen."

"I've heard talk," Amethyst said.

"Talk? What talk?" The other took her by the shoulders and peered up into her face. "What's to talk about?"

"Nothing. Heulwen died of the sickness, like her little sisters and poor Harcourt."

"And others recovered. The physician himself said I was as good as any apothecary he had ever met. You are not trying to tell me that my coltsfoot and honey made them worse!"

"It was talk, no more." Amethyst twisted away and reached up for the plates.

"Wicked talk," Mistress Gerthe said.

"People will say anything to fill up an empty hour," the girl said.

"If I hear any such talk I will nail it," Mistress Gerthe frowned. "Why, 'tis a dreadful thing to spread such a slander! Do they think I cannot tell one herb from another that I'd muddle up or brew the wrong quantities or something?"

"Slander is best ignored," Amethyst said. "They have nothing to do around here but talk about their betters. Anyway, there is no proof of anything."

"Proof of what?" Mistress Gerthe looked bewildered.

"Proof of nothing at all," Amethyst said, putting down the last plate and standing back to survey the effect.

The kitchen looked pleasant, with logs crackling on the hearth and the candles lit. Before long Will Bohanna would be the one to sit opposite her. Later there would be children, she supposed, but by then she hoped to be at 'Rowan Garth'. She had not been up to Pen Tân for some time and she made a mental resolve to ride over as soon as possible. She very much wanted to see Jan. The days when she did not see him were flat and featureless, but she particularly wanted to speak to him now. The pattern she was weaving required him to be part of it.

There was no need for her to ride over, as it chanced. The next morning she caught sight of the tall, broad-shouldered figure walking slowly towards the mill. She was already in her outdoor garments and ran to intercept him with lively, childlike pleasure in her face.

"I began to think you were at odds with us!" she exclaimed, linking her arm through his.

"I have not wished to leave Isobel alone," he returned sombrely. "She has been deeply depressed. Our first child."

So I don't really count, Amethyst thought. Probably they would have been much happier if I had been the one who died. I remind them of their youthful folly and now they are respectably wed I am an embarrassment.

"I have been meaning to ride over," she said brightly, "but I have not wished to leave Mistress Gerthe."

"My mother is not ill, is she?" he asked in swift alarm.

"No, quite well, but she seems – older suddenly," Amethyst said, knitting her smooth brow.

"She is past sixty," he pointed out, looking amused.

"She forgets things," Amethyst said.

"Forgets things?" he echoed. "What kind of things?"

"Oh, silly things. Like putting sugar in the stew instead of salt and never knowing where her spectacles are. She frets about it so I try not to mention it. I go around picking up things she has forgotten to put away or changing them around when she's put them in the wrong place. So I fear that if I leave her for too long I'll come back to find she's baking my boots and put the loaves in the shoe cupboard."

She laughed as she spoke, wrinkling her short, straight nose.

"My mother was never wont to be forgetful," Jan said, looking troubled. "Would you like me to have a word with her?"

"Pray don't! It would hurt her terribly if she thought people had begun to comment on how muddled she is getting," Amethyst said earnestly. "I only mentioned it to explain why I have not been up to 'Rowan Garth'."

"What my mother needs is a reliable servant-girl to come in every day," Jan said.

"She won't hear of it."

"I know. She likes to do everything herself. It was the same when I was a boy."

"Tell me about when you were a boy," Amethyst said. She loved to hear him talk about the neat, shining house in Flanders where he had grown up, the apprenticeship he had served, the quiet security of his life until the Spaniards had burned his father for heresy and he and Mistress Gerthe had fled into exile. She loved to hear him about anything as long as it kept him by her side. He seldom lingered, however, and this day was no exception.

"I have work to do. I've been neglecting the mill these past weeks. It sets a bad example to the men."

You neglected me for fifteen years, Amethyst thought bitterly. I didn't even know that you were my father. And you neglect me now, leaving me at Foster Farm with your stupid old mother.

"I shall be sixteen at Midsummer," she said.

"So you will." He had drawn away from her but now he turned to look at her. There were faint lines at the corners of his brown eyes as if he gazed across an endless vista of years.

"I shall be thinking of marrying soon, I dare say," she said, and saw his eyes narrow slightly, his wide mouth tighten.

"You are still very young," was all he said but his reaction had satisfied her. Just as she could not think of him as her father so, she guessed, he found it hard to think of her as a daughter. Something unspoken trembled in the air between them and was broken as he said heartily,

"Well, don't run off to be married yet! And now I've work to do. I'll look in on my mother before I ride back."

And I will stay out of sight, Amethyst thought. I will make you miss my presence as I miss yours in the empty days when you don't come. She walked back sedately to the house, resisting the temptation to turn and watch him stride into the mill.

"Was that Jan you were talking to?" Mistress Gerthe enquired, meeting her at the door.

Always spying! Amethyst clenched her fists and answered placidly,

"He said that he would call in before he returned to 'Rowan Garth'. I think I will saddle Cariad and go for a ride."

It was a relief to gallop day after day across the fields. The corn was already high, the meadows drowned in cowslips and buttercups, the sheep clambering sure-footed over the higher rocks, the slate cliffs purple blue in the sunlight. She spent hours alone, seldom troubling to interrupt Will at his labours, never bothering to go to 'Rowan Garth'. Her home no longer seemed like her home, with Isobel and Jan installed there like two turtle-doves.

The whispers were growing. It was possible the stable-lad had passed on the titbit she had fed him or that Will had puzzled over her hints. She had no way of knowing but what was very plain was that nobody now came for any of Mistress Gerthe's remedies and that after church on Sunday, when the congregation paused to exchange news and civilities, there were uneasy smiles and sidelong glances. She wondered how long it would be before enquiries were made, before the cause of Heulwen Evans's death was investigated more fully. There was danger in waiting too long. Mistress Gerthe might demand to be accused, might easily convince people she was neither careless nor criminal. The pattern that Amethyst was weaving might unravel in her hands.

At night she slept fitfully, the problem still resolving in her mind. April was blossoming into May and the sun was brilliant, tanning her skin to honey even though there were dark shadows under her eyes.

The answer when it came was simple and it was provided by Mistress Gerthe herself, Amethyst kept her few meetings with Will Bohanna as discreet as possible. There were no more passionate kisses, only a few words and a brief handclasp. She thought it wiser to leave him still a trifle uncertain. The day when he would take her for granted was a long way ahead if Amethyst had anything to do with it. Instead of making certain that she was constantly with him, she appeared when he least expected her, talked commonplaces while her eyes talked of other things and tickled his palm with the tips of her slender fingers while her lips denied the possibility of a kiss. She left him a little more bound to her each time that she left him, and the knowledge gave her an added sense of power.

She had been riding up to the high crags one day and had come home after the brief spring twilight.

"Home." She muttered the word, her lips curling, as she led Cariad to her stall, the lad had gone home; Jan and Isobel were at home; she was condemned to return to Foster Farm, and the farm was a property she owned, never home.

She rubbed Cariad down, delaying the moment when she would have to go through to the kitchen. Mistress Gerthe would be there, laying the table for supper, her mouth pursed and her spectacles slipping to the end of her nose. Passionately the girl wished that when she entered the house Jan would be sitting by the fire, his feet on the hearthstone, a mug of ale in his hand. She had seen him thus once or twice but his mother had been there too, and now and again, forgetting her presence, they had broken into Flemish. If only they could be there together with no third person to disturb them or come between!

She patted Cariad's velvety nose and went across to the back door. The window was shuttered against the night air and there was a moment's pause after her sharp rap before the bolt was drawn back and Mistress Gerthe opened the door.

"Why was it locked?" Amethyst asked in surprise.

"Because it's after dark and I won't leave the house at the mercy of burglars," Mistress Gerthe said.

"Burglars! You never locked up against them before," Amethyst exclaimed, pulling off her hat and shaking her curls free.

"You never came home so late before," the other said sharply. "If it happens again I have a good mind to keep you on the other side of the door until you've learned your lesson, young lady!"

Amethyst had paled slightly and her hands were shaking but she kept her voice low and calm.

"This is my house, my door. I come and go as I choose."

"Not until you're a woman grown. I've warned you before – "

"Over and over! I am sick of your lectures, your fault-finding, your interference!"

"Where have you been?" Mistress Gerthe interrupted. "Have you been with the Bohanna lad again?"

"I've been riding. Alone."

"Until this hour? It's close on eight of the clock."

"I like to ride alone," Amethyst said, taking off her cloak. "There's no law against riding alone."

"But you have been seeing William Bohanna, haven't you? I've no doubt people are already talking about your conduct. Wanton, aren't you? That's the truth of the matter!"

"I see Will now and then," Amethyst said sullenly. "Why shouldn't I see him? Am I not allowed to have friends?"

"You never sought them before," Mistress Gerthe said.

"Well, now I do want friends. Why do you make such a fuss?"

"Because I am responsible for you and because you gave me your word," Mistress Gerthe said implacably. "I intend to inform Jan of your conduct. I warned you that I would if you persisted in your bad behaviour. Will Bohanna is a good man, I'm sure, but you are too young to flaunt yourself across the countryside, and certainly too young to tie yourself to anyone without your family's knowledge and approval."

Amethyst had gone so pale that her tan looked yellowish in the firelight but her eyes glittered a hard and brilliant blue.

"I truly was riding alone," she said, wetting her lips. "Truly."

"It makes no matter. You have no right to stay out after dark and fret me so! It is not the behaviour of a modest, well-reared young girl."

"I was never well reared," Amethyst muttered, but the other ignored her.

"Whatever else, I intend to inform Jan. In my opinion you need a firmer hand. You have been left to run wild for too long, and if this state of affairs is allowed to continue then you will become the talk of the neighbourhood. People will say the bad blood is coming out in you. No! You need not make me any more promises. They are quite useless, I fear. Perhaps Jan will be able to talk some sense of decorum into you. There is no point in your sulking or in our being bad friends. You must learn to accept a rebuke gracefully."

"I'll make the tea." Amethyst took the key hanging on its peg by the door and went into the pantry.

The expensive and, in Amethyst's view, overrated black leaves were locked away for safe keeping in a carved wooden box in the pantry. Jan had bought a pound of the tea on a visit to Chester to sell cloth and it was doled out on rare occasions. No doubt Mistress Gerthe wished to mollify her a little. The girl's face twisted into a grimace of contempt but her hands were still shaking. She could deal with the old woman but she would die of shame if she were forced to listen to Jan scolding her as if she were a naughty child. She could not bear it if Jan believed for one moment that she had behaved wantonly. She could not win his love but she craved his good opinion.

Her hands were suddenly quite steady as she reached up to the shelf. The worst crime in the world was to waste the perfect opportunity and then spend the rest of her life regretting it.

There was a raised pork pie for supper, and bread with raisins in it, and an apple tart. Long after the memory of that evening had faded Amethyst could recall in detail the food laid on the table. She could not remember actually brewing the steaming beverage but she had only to close her eyes to see the firelight glinting on Mistress Gerthe's spectacles and the shadow of the little Flemish woman thrown by the candle-flames across the shutters.

"It gives me no pleasure to scold you," Mistress sat, bending to cut the raisin bread into neat, thin slices. "I hoped that we would get along comfortably together, but that is quite impossible while you continue defiant."

"I am not defiant," Amethyst said.

"Not now you have been scolded, but I intend to inform Jan all the same."

"You must do as you choose," Amethyst said.

She spoke gently, almost indifferently, as she stirred the boiling liquid.

# Four

The inquest was being held in the church, this being the only public building of any size in the neighbourhood. And what was clearer than anything was that everybody in the neighbourhood intended to attend.

Amethyst, sitting next to Isobel, kept her eyes lowered as the pews filled up and the Coroner, who had ridden over from Caernarvon, rapped his gavel sharply. Gossip was rife, running like fever from house to house. Mistress Gerthe had taken poison out of remorse. Mistress Gerthe had killed poor Heulwen Evans and her two sisters, though nobody was quite sure of her reasons for so doing. Mistress Gerthe had been secretly in league with the devil for years. Every new rumour was a little wilder than the last.

The proceedings began and it was immediately clear that the Coroner was a man who considered proven fact more important than the most convoluted speculations. Thin-faced and bewigged, rubbing his fingers together from time to time with a dry, rasping sound, he seemed determined to reduce everything to the barest and most uninteresting account.

Mistress Gerthe Schneider, widow, died suddenly after

drinking a dish of the beverage known as tea. The dregs of the tea were examined by the physician, who found the mixture to contain a large quantity of henbane and deadly nightshade. There was no argument as to how Mistress Gerthe had met her death. The physician, confined to laymen's terminology by the Coroner, gave his evidence in a brisk fashion.

Amethyst heard her name called and rose, making her way quietly to the stool that had been placed for witnesses. She seated herself, raising her eyes briefly to scan the rows of dark-clad people ranged in front of her. She had put on a mourning dress of untrimmed wool and a black veil subdued her vivid hair.

"Mistress Amethyst Prester, you lived with Mistress Gerthe Schneider?"

"This past year, since my mother married Jan Schneider," she nodded.

"And your relationship with Mistress Gerthe Schneider was a friendly one?"

"Oh, yes," she answered softly. "I was beginning to be very fond of her."

"Will you tell us exactly what happened on the night Mistress Schneider died?"

Amethyst took a deep breath, fixed her eyes on the Coroner's thin face, and began to speak, her voice sweet and clear.

"I went out riding and was a little late returning. Mistress Gerthe was anxious about me and a little flustered, but she had kept supper back and when I got in she brewed some tea. We had our supper and then I went upstairs to bed. I was tired after my ride. I woke up earlier than usual, probably because I'd been to bed early, and I was surprised to find the candles burned right down to their sockets when I opened my door and looked out on the landing. Mistress Gerthe dowsed all the lights when she came to bed."

"Go on." The Coroner nodded encouragement as she hesitated.

"I dressed and went down into the kitchen. The candles were burnt out there too, and Mistress Gerthe was sitting with her head on the table. I thought she was asleep and I went over and shook her and she didn't move. She didn't move and I couldn't hear her breathing. I ran out to the stable and saddled up Cariad and rode down the valley to fetch Master Prys."

"The physician?"

"Yes, sir. He came back with me at once and said that she was dead. He said that it looked like a heart attack but I told him that Mistress Gerthe was a healthy woman. She never ailed save for a little cold now and then."

"Who thought it might be poison?"

"Dr Prys said it was possible. He said he thought it might have been the pork pie that was not fresh, but I had eaten it and felt perfectly well. Then I remembered that I had not drunk any of the tea."

"Why not?" he interposed.

"I don't like the taste of tea very much," she said simply.

"I see. Pray continue." The Coroner made a note.

"He took what was left of the brew away with him. Then I went to Pen Tân to tell them there."

"From what the good physician has told us there is absolutely no doubt that Mistress Schneider died from the effects of the poisonous substances in the brew. Can you offer any possible explanation as to how it came to be there?"

"The leaves of tea were locked away," Amethyst said. "Mistress Gerthe unlocked the casket herself and put the leaves into the pot."

"A pot kept especially for that purpose?"

"Why, no. Just a pot, sir."

"In which other substances could have been mixed?"

"I suppose so. Yes, it wasn't kept especially for the brewing of tea," Amethyst said slowly.

"Mistress Gerthe was something of a herbalist, was she not?"

"Yes, sir. She collected herbs and made them into simples and tisanes."

"Including henbane and deadly nightshade?"

"I scarcely know one plant from another," Amethyst confessed. "She put down stuff to kill the rats sometimes."

"Could she have mixed it in the pot where she later brewed the tea?"

"I suppose so. She usually washed everything carefully but recently – "

"Recently what?" the Coroner prompted.

"She had been forgetful, a mite muddled," Amethyst said. Her voice was reluctant, her expression one of dawning distress. "I mentioned it to Master Schneider. She put sugar in the stew once or twice and on one occasion she dressed herself for church and would have gone had I not reminded her that it was only Saturday."

"Are you suggesting she was losing her mind?"

"Oh, no, sir! She was becoming a little forgetful, that is all and her sight was not as it had been. There was some talk of her having given Heulwen Evans the wrong physic."

"Talk is not evidence and we are not here to investigate the death of Mistress Evans," the Coroner said severely.

"No, sir." Rebuked, she flushed delicately and felt a ripple of sympathy run through the crowded pews.

"One more question." The Coroner rasped his fingers together. "Can you tell us what mood Mistress Schneider was in when you saw her on that last evening?"

"As usual," Amethyst said, her brow wrinkling slightly. "Save that she was a little flustered and anxious because I was late in coming home."

"Thank you. That is all."

Dismissed she resumed her seat next to Isobel.

"It seems to me," the Coroner said, rasping his fingers together again, "that the facts here are simple and bear only one cogent interpretation. Mistress Gerthe Schneider had lived here for nearly twenty years and was a well-respected member of the community. She was also a devout Christian, a Huguenot who had already suffered persecution for her faith and been exiled from her own land. She was the last person to have taken her own life and as she had no enemies there is no question of her having been killed unlawfully by any other person or persons. There remains the possibility that her death was an accident and this is the possibility I am inclined to favour, not because it is a likely possibility but because the evidence tends to support it. Mistress Schneider was elderly, her sight and her memory were beginning to fail although, like many elderly people, she would not admit it."

He paused but every eye was fixed upon him in breathless attention.

"It has been suggested that Mistress Gerthe had already muddled the ingredients in one of her physics, thus causing the death of one, Heulwen Evans. Talk and rumour are not evidence, but the possibility that such an error could have been made must weigh in the balance. Now, we come to the night on which Mistress Schneider died. We have been told by Mistress Amethyst Prester that the old lady was in a state of agitation due to Mistress Amethyst's coming home later than usual. She brewed some tea in a pot which was not kept especially for that purpose. It is probable that whatever was previously mixed in that pot had not been properly washed out. We have been told that Mistress Schneider had mixed stuff to keep away the rats. She may have mixed it in the same pot where later she brewed the tea, and it is also probable that her agitation of mind contributed to her mistake. I am therefore recording a verdict of 'Accident'. Thank you for your attention.''

He rasped sharply with his gavel and the pews began to empty slowly. Amethyst pulled her veil over her face and came out, a little behind Isobel and Jan. Neighbours were offering renewed condolences and Isobel was clinging to Jan's arm. He looked pale beneath his tan and strained as if he had not yet come to terms with the reality of his mother's death. Several people wrung his hand sympathetically.

"You must return home with us," he said, turning to Amethyst.

Hope clutched at her heart and then withdrew its grasp. To return to 'Rowan Garth' would mean having to watch Jan and Isobel together, to become the daughter of the house again with two parents instead of one.

"I would prefer to stay at Foster Farm," she said.

"Don't be ridiculous!" Isobel said sharply. "A maid who is not yet sixteen cannot possibly live alone."

"Foster Farm is my house," the girl said.

"And the mill is your mill but nobody expects you to run it alone," Jan said kindly.

"I was thinking of engaging a servant to live in with me," Amethyst said. "Naturally, I wouldn't expect to live entirely by myself."

"You and a flighty servant-girl!" Isobel said crossly. "I thought – perhaps an older woman. Liza Jenkins is past forty and new widowed. She will lose her cottage now that her husband is gone."

Isobel hesitated. Perhaps, after all, it would be more comfortable if Amethyst remained at Foster Farm. It was so peaceful at 'Rowan Garth' with only Jan there, and the memory of little Harcourt to be a shared sadness between them. Amethyst was a reminder of past shame and her bright youth contrasted too greatly with Isobel's fading blonde charms.

"I am sure Mistress Jenkins would be grateful," Amethyst murmured.

"Very well, then. I will speak to her first thing in the morning," Isobel decided.

"And I may spend tonight at Foster Farm? I truly would like to be alone there," Amethyst pleaded.

"Mistress Jenkins will come over tomorrow," Isobel said.

Amethyst waited hopefully for Jan to say he would ride down to check that she had locked up but he was handing Isobel to her horse and there was unmistakable relief on his face. So Jan didn't really want her at 'Rowan Garth' either. Amethyst pulled her veil lower and shed the first genuine tears since Mistress Gerthe's death. She had never felt so unwanted and so alone.

"I do pray you not to weep," Will Bohanna murmured, moving to her side.

He wore a band of black crêpe round his hat, something which obscurely irritated her. Mistress Gerthe, after all had been no relative of his!

"I was very fond of her, for all her interfering ways," she said sadly.

"It is near Midsummer." He looked at her hopefully.

"So?"

"You said that at Midsummer – " .

"But we shall be in full mourning now until August. One cannot make an announcement under such circumstances."

"But people are dying all the time," Will argued. They had stepped to the gate and he stood aside to let her go through first.

"A few weeks can make no difference," Amethyst said softly. "We will have the summer, Will, to keep our secret a little longer. I never had a secret with anyone before."

"You have not altered your mind?" he enquired anxiously.

"Not in the least." She gazed at him gently, her face a pale pearl under the dark meshes of the veil. "I will never alter my opinion of you, Will."

He was strong and comely and she had convinced him that he was in love with her. He would make a good husband, but she was glad the matter would be delayed a while. She was still not ready to give herself completely to any man save the one she could not have.

But it was good to be alone at Foster Farm. She had never had a whole house to herself before and, though the place would never be as dear to her as 'Rowan Garth', it was still her property. When she had stabled Cariad she walked slowly through the neat and primly furnished rooms. Mistress Gerthe's clothes and her few possessions had been packed away, her bed stripped, even her chamber-pot scaled and placed in the cupboard. There was nothing to remind anyone of the little Flemish woman, and Amethyst thought of her scarcely at all save as something else that had been tidily packed away. Now she walked through the rooms, touching each piece of furniture lightly, bouncing on the yellow counterpane in the blissful knowledge that nobody was there to scold her. She could tread mud over the floors and come home as late as she pleased. She could behave in any way she chose and there would be only Liza Jenkins to object. Amethyst pulled off her veil and smiled at herself in the glass. She had no doubt that she could deal with Liza Jenkins.

That night she slept well for the first time in months, her cheek pillowed on her hand, her curls rumpled against the white pillow. If any ghosts walked in the kitchen below she was unaware of them and all her dreams were peaceful.

Mistress Jenkins arrived the next morning. She was a thin, frizzy-haired little woman with a sad, apologetic manner and eyes as grateful as a spaniel's. Her husband had been a shepherd but they had no children and his death had threatened her with eviction from the small cottage where they had lived.

"Such a fine house," she said, clasping work-worn hands before her as she gazed round the parlour. "Oh, it is very good of Master Schneider to offer me this opportunity! I shall take every care to give satisfaction, Mistress Amethyst."

"Did you bring your things with you?" Amethyst enquired.

"They are being sent over later in the day. I have very few belongings. Our lives were very simple – not that I cannot cook well if I have the right ingredients. Samuel, my late husband, always swore that my bread was the lightest he had ever tasted. Good plain sewing too, though I never learned the art of fine needlework."

"I am sure we will suit very well together," Amethyst smiled. "I am most easy to please."

"Such a sad event," Liza Jenkins said. "I don't believe I ever spoke to Mistress Gerthe, but I knew her by sight, of course. A terrible accident."

"Terrible indeed, but we must not dwell on past griefs," Amethyst said. "Come and see your room. It is the smaller of the two, but you will find it comfortable, I hope."

Mistress Jenkins was one of those people who find everything comfortable and repeat the fact over and over again. She was unfailingly grateful for her new home and expressed her gratitude over and over until Amethyst was wearied of it. She was, however, a good cook and cleaned the house without pointing out that it was Amethyst who caused most of the mess. One could grow quite fond of her in time, Amethyst decided, smiling as the little housekepper repeated yet again that the view from her bedroom window was glorious.

"She is one of the most tedious women I ever met in my life," Amethyst confided to Jan when he came down to the mill one day.

"Poor Amethyst!" He smiled at her but his smile was preoccupied and didn't reach his eyes.

"Is anything wrong?" she asked, sensitive to his every nuance.

"Your mother is with child again," he said, "and very far from well. We had planned a supper-party to mark your sixteenth birthday but Isobel is not up to entertaining."

"She must not think of it!" Amethyst exclaimed over the lump that was forming in her throat. "We are still in mourning anyway! Any celebration can easily be postponed."

"Thank you, my dear." He reached out to take her hand and let it go immediately, a dull red staining his cheekbones.

"When is the babe due?" she asked.

"Not until January if all goes well."

So he and her mother had assuaged their grief for Harcourt in each other's arms.

"I will ride over and see her in a day or two," she said.

"You are not lonely at Foster Farm?" He shot her a quick, enquiring glance.

"You never asked me that before," she said.

"Ah, my mother was alive and provided company. Mistress Jenkins does not, I think, do that."

"You should visit me more often." She gave him her dimpling smile but he stepped away stiffly.

"Your mother needs me."

He felt the tug between them too, Amethyst thought, staring after him. He didn't have fatherly feelings just as she didn't have daughterly ones. She wondered if he thought of her when Isobel was in his arms.

"Give her my love," she called after him. "It will be good to have a babe in the family again."

A babe to inherit Pen Tân which would have come to me if my parents had married at the right time. She wanted to be sick but she waved her hand gaily, watching him go.

That night, after supper, she found herself moving restlessly about the kitchen. The light had not faded and the yard was bathed in mellow sunshine. Mistress Jenkins sat by the fire with mending in her lap and her head bent industriously. She was capable of sitting like that for hours, never speaking save when she was addressed. Amethyst, glancing at her, said impatiently,

"Put your work away and let us talk a while."

"If you wish." The housekeeper folded her work neatly and laid it aside.

"We'll have some malmsey. Do you like malmsey?" Amethyst went to the dresser where goblets and wine jar stood.

"I don't think I ever tasted it, mistress," the other said. "Sam and I never drank aught but ale or cider, and I used to have mine well watered. I've a bit of a weak head for drink, if the truth be told."

"Malmsey cannot hurt you." Amethyst poured a generous measure and presented it with a flourish. For lack of more congenial entertainment it might be amusing to test the weakness of the housekeeper's head.

"It tastes very rich." Mistress Jenkins sipped, then drank more deeply.

"Rich and smooth." Amethyst took her own measure and went to sit opposite. "We will drink a toast."

"To what, mistress?"

"I am sixteen in a few days. Doesn't that merit a toast?"

"To your birthday then, mistress."

The goblets were tipped and drained and Amethyst went back to the dresser to fill them again.

"Sixteen years. Time passes," Mistress Jenkins said,

accepting the second drink. "I remember when you were born. Sam and I had been wed not long before and I recall him saying that we would have one of our own in due course. We never did, alas!"

Sighing, she drank the malmsey and hiccupped gently.

"And in January there will be a new babe," Amethyst said. "My mother is expecting again. So we will drink a toast to the newcomer!"

"To the new babe." Mistress Jenkins drank deeply and shook her head slightly, blinking her pale eyes. "My, what a strange thing life is! Nobody ever thought that Master Schneider would finally wed Mistress Isobel. Mind, he never would have done if Master Cassian had lived."

"We do not speak of my uncle," Amethyst said carefully.

"And who can doubt that it's wise to say nothing!" Mistress Jenkins cried. "Such men ought to be forgotten. Oh, but it's a wicked, unnatural act to corrupt one's own sister!"

"Yes. Yes, it is." Amethyst sat very still, her eyes fixed on the other's face.

"But you were born without blemish," the housekeeper said, taking another mouthful of malmsey. "They say such children are born mad, but you were a perfect child. It was hard on Mistress Isobel. She shut herself away for years and Master Schneider lived at this house with his mother and we none of us imagined we would ever be asked to drink to their wedded bliss! Life is strange."

"And my – father had died," Amethyst said. Her hands were clasped so tightly about her goblet of malmsey that her fingers were cramped, but her voice was calm.

"Hanged himself from one of the rowan trees up at Pen

Tân," the other nodded and hiccupped again. "Why, you might be called the rowan maid!"

"So I might," Amethyst said.

"Not that the matter is ever talked about," Mistress Jenkins said. "There's many who don't know the truth and those who do – we have too much respect for Mistress Isobel to gossip. Silence – is golden."

"Silence is golden," Amethyst said.

"We were drinking a toast. What were we drinking a toast about?"

"To the babe. The one that will be born in January."

"Dear little soul." Mistress Jenkins looked hopefully towards the dresser.

"I have a weak head for the drink," the housekeeper said. "I say more than I ought. Master Schneider – did I say that right? 'Tis a hard name, but he's Dutch or some such thing."

"Flemish."

"A good man for all that. Good to take you as a daughter. Everybody admired him for that! Least said – I forget the rest of it but 'tis very true."

She wagged her finger roguishly, her voice slurring a little.

"Better have a rest. You look sleepy," Amethyst said, taking the goblet out of the other's hand.

"Forty winks." Mistress Jenkins yawned and leaned back. Her mouth hung open and in a few moments a gentle snoring escaped her.

Amethyst rose like a sleepwalker and took the goblets over to the stone sink to rinse them. She felt unreal as if at any moment she might shatter into pieces. Jan Schneider was not her true father. In the deepest part of herself she had always known it. It was Cassian, the uncle nobody ever talked about, the uncle who was buried separately from the rest of the family. It was Cassian, Isobel's brother who had fathered her.

"I am the child of incest," she said aloud.

The phrase had a biblical ring that pleased her.

She dried the goblets and put them back on the dresser, setting them gently into place, moving slowly and carefully so as not to lose her control. If she let herself go she would laugh without ceasing until the sanity was all squeezed out of her and she was nothing but crazy laughter. It was wiser to be angry, coldly, silently angry. Isobel and Jan had lied to her. He had never been her true father at all. If he and Isobel had not met again after fifteen years then it was likely he would have fallen in love with and married Amethyst instead.

"Heavens! have I been asleep?" Mistress Jenkins jerked upright in her chair, shaking her head in a bemused fashion.

"You dropped off for a moment," Amethyst said.

"It was the wine. I am not used to such strong wine," Mistress Jenkins said muzzily. "Sam used to tease me about it when he was alive – not that we could afford such wine! Ale and cider were all we bought and those well watered! It is most kind of you to offer such rich fare. We were talking of babies, I seem to remember."

"Of the one to be born in January," Amethyst said.

"Bless its little heart," said Mistress Jenkins and fell asleep again.

# Five

"First reaping will be upon us soon," Will Bohanna said.

He spoke in a dreary, reflective manner but there was a question in his eyes as he glanced at Amethyst.

Affecting to ignore it, she said brightly, "And such a fine summer as we've had should mean good crops. My mother is doubtless pleased with your stewardship."

"So pleased that if I asked her permission now I'm sure she'd grant it," he said.

"Permission? Permission for what, Will?" she enquired.

"Why, for us to be wed." He turned his gaze from the gleaming corn and stared at her in surprise.

"Wed?" Amethyst stared back at him blankly.

"You're past sixteen now and your time of mourning is nearly over. Mistress Isobel would be pleased – "

"You didn't take our game seriously, did you?" she asked, lifting her brows.

"Game?"

"Game of courtship. You never took it seriously?"

"Of course I did. You made it very plain that you favoured me!"

"Oh Lord! that was only funning!" Amethyst cried. "You

couldn't have imagined that I meant it!"

"You did mean it. You kissed me and talked of marriage."

"If every couple who kissed and talked of marriage actually wed the land would be full of bigamists," she said.

"But this was not just talk! You meant what you said."

"Oh, I often don't mean all that I say," Amethyst said lightly. "Except now, of course. I do mean what I say now."

"But it was you who first spoke of marriage!"

"And you thought I meant it? You cannot have imagined I am so badly reared as to fling myself at a boy?"

"But we talked of getting wed," he said blankly.

"You do repeat yourself," Amethyst said critically. "People of small education are apt to repeat themselves."

"We were not talking of my education but of marriage."

"You are talking of marriage! I am not talking of anything," she said, pulling a stalk of grass and chewing it. "I thought we were good friends, you and I. Why spoil it with talk of wedlock?"

"You mentioned it first," Will said obstinately.

"As a jest."

"It was no jest," he interrupted, catching at her hand. "You must think me a fool if you expect me to believe that! You have changed your mind about me. Cannot you be honest enough to say so?"

"Let me be! I hate to be grabbed!" she said crossly, snatching her hand away.

"But you were the one who – "

"Oh, do hush!" She turned upon him, fury in her face. "It is like a man to heap all the blame upon a woman. I was funning and if you took it seriously that isn't my fault! You must sort it out with yourself."

"I am not well treated," he began.

"Not well treated! At nineteen you are steward of a prosperous farm. You own your own house and land. I am your friend. How are you not well treated?"

"You seek to make a fool of me."

"You must be a fool already if you could believe I really wanted to marry you," Amethyst said. "It was a jest!"

"Then you may jest alone," Will said sullenly, "for I'll not sit by and be your target a moment longer!"

"As to that you may please yourself," she said and walked off to where Cariad was tethered, mounting without help and riding away without looking back.

Will stared after her, baffled and angry. He had not thought of loving her until she had kissed him in the churchyard and spoken of marriage. She had put the notion in his head and encouraged it to grow and now he felt a complete fool. His good-looking young face was dark with chagrin and he kicked moodily at the turf, sending clods of it flying up under the toe of his boot.

Amethyst felt a mixture of relief and regret as she rode away. She could not have endured to marry Will now, but a genuine affection for him had grown up in her. It had been pleasant to have a friend, to ride with him and talk and tease him a little. She had never had a friend and it would seem lonely if Will continued to be angry. She hoped that he would think better of it, but if not she was ready to go back to her old condition when she had always felt alone.

She rode on over the hill and saw beneath her the grey church huddling against the cliff. The yews were dark in the sunshine and she glimpsed the stooped figure of the minister bending over the rose border that gladdened the turf along the edge of the cemetery. The Reverend Elias was a man whom the girl disliked, for she sensed that he disapproved of her and that, given his own way, he would spend a good part of his time in lecturing her. Today, however, she was glad to see him. Before she felt free to act as she wished, she had to be absolutely certain.

Dismounting at the gate she walked slowly up the path, raising her voice in greeting.

"Good morrow, Master Elias! Isn't it a beautiful day?"

"A very fine afternoon, mistress." He straightened up from his roses and turned his dark, critical gaze upon her.

"I have been riding," she said unnecessarily. "It's a good feeling to ride over the hills."

"And a better one to work hard," he said. "Work is a gift from the Lord. I do not like to see idle hands in young people."

"I am often idle," Amethyst said sadly. "I sometimes think it is the bad blood in me."

"Bad blood?" Master Elias looked at her sharply. "My father … " she began in a low voice.

"Master Schneider is a most worthy, God-fearing man for all that he is a foreigner."

"Jan Schneider is not my real father," Amethyst said. "My mother's brother, Cassian, was."

She knew by the start the clergyman gave that Mistress Jenkins had spoken truly even before he said, "Who told you this?"

"Vague rumours, talk that breaks off in the middle when I appear. I came to ask you for the truth."

"It was agreed that nothing should be said, to spare your mother and yourself further pain."

"It is more painful to me not to know," Amethyst said, her eyes earnest.

"You have not spoken to your mother or to Master Schneider?"

"I thought it best to come to you."

"In that you displayed good sense," he approved. "It's a terrible tale, and in my own opinion, best forgotten, but since you have heard part, then you shall hear all."

"Yes, Master Elias?" She fixed him with a sweet, expectant gaze, her narrow hands clasped.

"Your grandmother, Mistress Mina, was widowed before her twins were born. She reared them without any masculine help, for she had no relatives of her own and her husband, Walter, had been the last of the Presters. It was not an easy task to bring up a family without a husband and Mistress Mina doted over them too much."

"On my uncle, Cassian and my mother, Isobel?"

Master Elias nodded.

"Isobel was a sweet, timid, biddable girl, devoted to her twin. Sibling affection is a righteous thing save when it twists into perversity. In Cassian the natural love he bore his sister became an unnatural, ungodly thing. We none of us guessed at it because he hid it beneath a cloak of concern for her well-being. It is my private conviction that it never would have broken out if she had remained unwed, but Jan Schneider came with his mother to manage the mill at Foster Farm and he and Isobel fell in love."

"And Cassian objected to the match?"

"Not openly. Oh, it was not a brilliant match but Jan Schneider was already winning respect for the way in which he was managing the mill and for his excellent moral character. I was pleased to hear of the betrothal."

"Then what happened?" Amethyst said sharply. She had no wish to hear any more about the affection that had sprung up between Jan and her mother.

"The betrothal was broken off and no reason given," Master Elias said. "It was sad and puzzling but I advised Master Schneider to be patient. Young girls often take fright just before their marriages, and patience is needed. But Isobel came to the Sunday service not many weeks later and sat upon the penance stool."

"What!" Amethyst stared at him, her mouth open. The penance seat was reserved for adulterous wives, maids who got themselves into trouble, boys who had indulged in poaching or petty thieving. She could not imagine her delicate, shy mother doing such a thing.

"From the penance stool she accused her brother of raping her and leaving her with child. Cassian fled before anyone could lay hands on him and hanged himself from one of the rowan trees near 'Rowan Garth'."

"And was buried separate from the rest," Amethyst said slowly.

"We could not lay him in consecrated ground," Master Elias said. "You were born and after that your mother confined herself to Pen Tân land and never went near Foster Farm. It was agreed that you should be told nothing about your father. One does not wish an innocent child to suffer. But the Lord works in mysterious ways. Your mother and Jan Schneider were reconciled and he gallantly assumed responsibility for your begetting. In a generation the ugly truth will be quite forgotten and nobody will question that you are Jan Schneider's daughter."

"I am a bastard, born of incest," she said flatly.

"Mistress, if you are wise you will put that knowledge out of your head," he said sternly. "Above all, don't hurt your mother by telling her you have discovered the truth. Mistress Isobel is in a delicate condition, as you know, and has already had much trouble this year. The death of her babe and the death of Mistress Gerthe were both sad events for her and for Master Schneider."

"I ought never to have been born," Amethyst said.

"That is foolish talk!" Master Elias said. "You are a fortunate girl, to have a mill and a house of your own, to have kind parents who are devoted to you and wish to save you from hurt. I am not of the opinion that any child is born evil. Your nature may derive from your father but it derives also from your mother, who is a sweet and gentle lady. Take her as your model, my dear, and accept Jan Schneider as your father. I know he is fond of you for your mother's sake."

"Thank you for telling me." She spoke meekly.

"Put old and ugly incidents out of your mind," he advised. "Strive to be a good maid and a credit to your parents. Forget Cassian, for his punishment must be an everlasting one. Attain virtue, mistress."

She nodded, her face still meek, her hands clasped so tightly that her bones felt as if they were about to snap.

"Well, I must get on." He gave her a faintly embarrassed glance and shuffled off.

Mistress Jenkins had spoken truly even though she had been drunk. In wine many truths were revealed.

"Cassian is my real father," Amethyst whispered, staring at an overblown rose that spilled prodigal petals at her feet.

"Cassian was both my uncle and my father. Jan was never my father at all!"

He might have married her instead of Isobel. He would have married her if he had not met Isobel again. It had been the worst possible fortune that Isobel had roused in him some echo of the boyish passion he had once felt for her. Given only a little time he would have fallen in love with Amethyst. There was no bar to their loving and Jan must have known it all the time. For a moment blazing anger shot through her, but she could not endure to be angry with Jan for very long. It was clearly Isobel who had seduced him back into her arms because she could not bear to see the man she had once loved marrying her daughter. The anger chilled to ice and was turned towards Isobel. Amethyst, as she walked slowly back to where Cariad was tethered, knew that it would give her the greatest pleasure to kill Isobel. Murder, however, would afford her only a momentary satisfaction. A lasting revenge must be more subtle.

Mounting up, she rode back to Foster Farm, her brow so smooth as if no thought had ever troubled its placidity. Jan was due to come down this evening to go over the accounts with her. He came every month and the occasions were formal affairs. They sat at each side of the parlour table with the ledgers between them and Mistress Jenkins knitting by the fire. There had been a constraint in the atmosphere ever since he had married her mother. Tonight she would make certain that everything was different.

First, there was Mistress Jenkins to be dealt with. Her presence was certainly superfluous, the girl thought with a wry grin. In many ways she was becoming quite fond of the woman despite her garrulity and her endless protestations of gratitude. She kept the house spotless and her cooking, though plain, was more than adequate, and although she took her duties as chaperon very seriously she never questioned Amethyst about her various comings and goings. A pinch of this and that in her supper would cause her to sleep heavily until morning. There was no sense in hurting someone unless it was absolutely necessary.

"May we have supper early tonight?" She raised her voice slightly as she went into the kitchen.

"Certainly, Mistress Amethyst. I have two roast pigeons in the bake-oven and a goosegog tart. It will be ready whenever you wish."

"I shall make a caper sauce to go with the pigeons," Amethyst said brightly. "Mistress Gerthe taught me the recipe for it and praised the flavour most highly. I found it a trifle rich for my taste but I believe you will like it. We'll have some sherry wine with the meal. You will like that too."

"So very good of you," Mistress Jenkins fluttered. "I was never so well treated before, even when Sam was alive. Mind, we never had much money in those days so one could never blame him for the lack of luxuries. And now Sam is gone and I am living at Foster Farm. Such a turnabout!"

She was capable of going on in the same vein for hours. Amethyst left her to it and went into the pantry to get the capers and the other herbs she needed for the sauce.

Supper was an outwardly congenial affair, eaten before the long shadows of twilight purpled the fields. The distant sounds of laughter drifted through the open window as the weavers made their way home and the breeze was a warm, caressing thing. Amethyst, picking at her food, watching Mistress Jenkins from beneath lowered lids. The housekeeper was eating heartily, scraping the last of the sauce up with a piece of bread and taking generous swigs of the sherry wine in between mouthfuls. Other people's weaknesses could be turned to advantage, Amethyst thought, and wished Mistress Jenkins would hasten to sleep quickly and stop her ceaseless chattering about the advantages of her new position.

"A wonderful sauce, my dear Mistress Amethyst, though you have scarcely touched it, but you did say the flavour was a trifle rich for you. To think of you going to the trouble to prepare it for me. I tell you I scarcely know that I am born since I came to Foster Farm."

She paused, hand to her mouth to conceal a yawn.

"You work very hard for any small comforts you may have," Amethyst said. "You look tired."

"I must confess to feeling a mite sleepy. I fear I've drunk a little too much sherry wine," Mistress Jenkins said. "I must clear away and wash up. It will bestir me!"

She rose slightly unsteadily, and clutched the edge of the table.

"Dear Mistress Jenkins, why don't you go upstairs and lie down for a while?" Amethyst said quickly. "I fear you've overtired yourself sadly with looking after me. No sense in making yourself ill!"

"It's exceedingly good of you," the other said, shaking her head muzzily. "Perhaps for an hour or so."

"I'll call you," Amethyst said, stifling a chuckle as she watched the housekeeper making her way with conscious uprightness out of the kitchen.

From upstairs came the sound of the door opening and then closing. Mistress Jenkins was safely out of the way until morning. Amethyst, feeling virtuous, took the pan of hot water from the hob and washed up the dishes. The kitchen looked neat and clean by the time she had swept the floor and mended the fire, and she went briskly out to the yard to lock up the hens for the night and to secure the two horses in their stalls. More than once she went to the gate to look out but there was no sign of the tall, sun-dappled figure riding towards her along the track, and the fear that he might, after all, not come began to grow in her. She thrust it away and went back into the house and up the stairs to her own bedroom. Through the closed door of the housekeeper's room she could hear the rhythm of snoring.

There was rosewater in her ewer and she stripped off her gown and washed away the grime that clung to her from the yard and stables. She had a robe of thin blue wool, intended to wear for private leisure moments and she knotted its sash tightly round her slender waist, noting with pleasure that the wide neckline half revealed her creamy shoulders and dipped to the cleft between her high breasts. The sleeves of the robe widened at the wrist and the wool clung to her long legs. Brushing her short curls she smiled at herself in the glass, excitement rising in her as she contemplated her own beauty. The last time she had seen her mother, Isobel had been pale and lethargic, the bulkiness of the child she carried distorting her figure and producing puffiness about her face.

Jan was coming. Through the window she could hear hoofbeats along the track. She would know his horse in a thousand, she thought, laying down the brush and hurrying to open the front door. He had dismounted and tethered his horse to the gate and, as his eyes met her own slanting blue ones, she was conscious of the little shock of recognition that leaped between them.

"Mistress Jenkins went upstairs with a headache and begs to be excused," she said, leading the way into the parlour.

Chairs and ledgers were set ready and a fire on the hearth competed with the last golden rays of sun.

"She is not sick, is she?" he queried anxiously.

"Merely a headache. She took a sleeping draught. Will you take some wine?"

"A thimbleful. I promised Isobel I'd not be long. She craves my company in the evenings."

'And I crave your company at all times,' Amethyst thought, pouring wine for them both.

"You have the books ready. Good girl!"

Consciously businesslike, he sat down and drew one of the ledgers towards him, running his finger down the columns, reaching for ink and quill to make new entries.

"The mill prospers," he said after a few moments. "You are going to be a rich young lady. Mind, I'm of the opinion that the finest fleeces come from Pen Tân sheep, but your spinners and weavers are skilled. There is so much untapped talent hereabouts that it seems to me a false economy to sell raw fleeces along the borders when we can work it ourselves."

"I love you," Amethyst said. She had intended to work up to it gradually but the words were jerked out of her by some compulsion beyond reason.

"It is natural for a daughter to love her father." His voice had not changed but the pen shook, blotting the page.

"You are not my father," she said. "My Uncle Cassian fathered me."

"Where did you get that tale?" he asked sharply.

"Odds and ends of conversation and then Master Elias confirmed it."

"You have not told your mother that you know!"

Amethyst shook her head.

"It was hoped that you would never find out," he said. "It must have been a very great shock."

"It was a very great relief," she countered. "I thought it was wrong to love you in the way I do, but if we are not related there is no wrong in it at all."

"We are related by law. I am married to your mother."

"But not by blood. None of your blood flows in my veins. We are free to love," she said eagerly.

"It would be a most grievous sin," he said curtly.

"Wasn't it more of a sin to wed my mother when you loved me?" she challenged. "You don't love her! If you had truly loved her you'd not have waited fifteen years to marry!"

"My dear, how could you, at your age, begin to understand?" He laid down the quill and rose, coming to where she stood, outlined against the last flames of the sinking sun. "I fell in love with Isobel at the first moment of meeting her. I thought of her as the perfect woman, the ideal of purity and loveliness. You cannot imagine how a lad of twenty feels when he learns that his sweetheart is with child by her own brother, even if it was a rape. And Isobel refused to see me, refused to talk. For years we lived a mile apart, never meeting."

"But then you met me!" she interrupted.

"And liked you, though I had good reason to hate your origins."

"You were ready to fall in love with me."

"All men are attracted to the young and beautiful. I am a man like any other."

"And you would have married me if my mother had not come between us."

"Oh, my dear, it was never in my mind," he said. "Your mother is the only woman I have ever loved. I saw you as a reflection of her, but with a vitality that was your own. I could almost warm my hands at it, but as for loving – I never loved anyone but Isobel. And you only fancy that you love me, you know. I am far too old for you, Amethyst. In a little while I will be forty and you are scarce sixteen. There will be a young man for you, someone whose loyalties are not bound elsewhere and you will love them with a free heart. Then you will know the reality of love, not its pretence."

"It is no pretence!" Colour flamed in her face and tears of anger sparkled on her lashes. "I shall never love anyone else as long as I live. It is you who lie! You desire me. I can see it in your eyes."

"You are a lovely girl," he said. "A man would have to be inhuman not to desire you, but that is not loving, Amethyst. Loving is deeper and stronger and takes no count of the passing of the years. If I gave way to temptation you would be spoiled for any other man and I would return to Isobel with the taste of betrayal in my mouth. I must be sensible for both of us."

"I want you," she gasped out, but when she would have pulled him close he stepped back, reaching for his hat, his face and voice cold.

"I will return to the accounts when Mistress Jenkins is fully recovered. Be sure to lock up after I have gone."

He bowed slightly and walked out of the parlour, closing the door softly behind him. She stood where she was, the sunlight flashing on her serpent ring and dappling her hands with the colour of blood. She had never felt such an anguish of rejection even when he had married her mother. Then she had imagined him to be her father. Now he had made it clear that Isobel was the one he loved.

"I wish she was dead." The girl spoke the words aloud. Her voice was soft but the ring dripped more blood onto her fingers.

## Six

Revenge must be subtle if it is going to be sweet, but subtlety takes time and Isobel was nearly at the end of her seventh month of pregnancy. Amethyst, glancing at her mother's distended stomach, did calculations in her head. Premature birth was a hazard for parent and child. And, in winter, when it was hard to obtain fresh food, nursing mothers often suffered from fever and sickness.

"I shall be glad when Christmas is over," Isobel said, shifting restlessly.

She always felt a little restless when her daughter was by.

"It is not yet November!" Amethyst exclaimed.

"But it will be good to have the cold season almost over and the babe safely come."

"Do you want a boy or a girl?" the other enquired.

"A boy to be master of Pen Tân one day," Isobel said promptly, "though a little girl would be nice."

Amethyst wanted to shout at her that she already had a girl, but she smiled instead, rising to go over to the window. The garden glowed with the last scarlets and rusts of autumn and the leaves were thick on the path. There was the promise of frost in the wind.

"Shall we have a drink? Something hot to warm us up?" she asked aloud.

"Myfi is cleaning the bedrooms," Isobel began.

"I'll make it. Hot milk spiced with nutmeg and with a splash of sherry," Amethyst said. "Mistress Gerthe swore it was most beneficial."

"That's very good of you, dear." Isobel leaned back, trying to shift into a more comfortable position as the babe kicked vigorously. She would be very glad when this birth was safely accomplished. She was, after all, near forty and her muscles lacked the suppleness of a younger woman. There were days, too, when she felt plain and clumsy and on those occasions she would glance fearfully at Jan wondering if his passion was dwindling into kindness. Amethyst, slender and flame-haired, made her feel old.

Crossing the wide hall into the kitchen Amethyst compared 'Rowan Garth' to Foster Farm. Here the rooms were not only more numerous and much larger but infinitely more luxurious. The dresser gleamed with its weight of gold and silver and copper and bowls of sweet-scented herbs perfumed the air. The furniture was lovingly polished, the tapestries that excluded draughts from doors and windows were newly woven and the clock ticking in the corner was faced with crystal. All this would have been hers – might still be hers – if Isobel died without legitimate issue.

She heated milk, added honey, nutmeg and sherry, beat an egg into it and poured the foaming liquid into two silver tankards. From the drawstring bag at the waist of her gown she took the whitish powder in its phial and added it to one of the tankards. Pennyroyal had to be used in tiny, gradually increasing doses, but she feared that she was underestimating Isobel's resistance. By now she ought to have begun to miscarry, for Amethyst had been visiting Pen Tân fairly regularly for weeks.

"It will be company for my mother while you are busy with the harvest," she had said, blue eyes limpid as she gazed at Jan, and he had nodded, relief in his face. The scene between them had never been mentioned but the constraint remained. It was possible that Jan had convinced himself her declaration of love had been no more than a youthful folly. He would learn, after Isobel's death, the enduring quality of her daughter's affection.

"Here we are, then!" She carried the drinks through and gave one to Isobel. "That will cheer you up."

"Oh, I am not dispirited," Isobel assured her. "It is only that the waiting seems very long."

"It will seem as nothing when the babe is here," Amethyst said.

"I have everything ready," Isobel brightened slightly. "You know I gave poor little Harcourt's things away, because I couldn't bear to keep them, before I knew I was with child again. Only think, had he lived there would have been scarce a year between them."

"Almost like twins," Amethyst murmured.

"As you say." Isobel frowned slightly as if she were brushing away a memory.

"We are such a small family," Amethyst said. "Only the three of us, really."

It was amusing to talk in this fashion, knowing how, if she chose, she could shatter Isobel's happiness with a few well-chosen words. But if she gave way to temptation Jan would hear of it and think the less of her. She could not endure that he should think badly of her even for a moment.

"Jan is a good father," Isobel said, a pleading note in her voice.

"And a good husband too, I'm certain," Amethyst murmured.

"I wish you to enjoy the same happiness one day," Isobel said. "We must begin to cast about for a good husband for you. Someone who will be ready to take on the management of the mill. Jan works so hard at the affairs of Pen Tân that I wish him to enjoy some leisure and not have to spend his spare time in overseeing Foster Farm as well."

A husband to sit in the parlour and check the accounts. A husband to sleep beside her under the yellow counterpane in the big bed. Amethyst's mind closed against the picture. Jan's visits were rare and chaperoned but she clung to them as the only contact she still enjoyed with the man she loved.

"I am young still," she said. "I have no desire to rush into wedlock."

"And I have no desire to force you into anything," Isobel said hastily.

"After all, you waited until you were thirty-six before you married Jan Schneider."

She could not say 'my father' even to Isobel.

"There were reasons." Isobel finished her drink and grimaced slightly, looking into the dregs.

"I ought to have put more honey in it," Amethyst said. "Mine tasted a trifle bitter."

"I haven't much of an appetite these days," Isobel remarked.

"You should eat sufficient for two." Amethyst put down

her own tankard and said. "And I should be starting back."

"Will you not wait to see Jan?" Isobel asked.

"I ought to be getting back," Amethyst said. "Mistress Jenkins is apt to fret when she's alone in the house. I'll slip up to say goodbye to Myfi."

"You'll ride over again soon?"

"In a week or two." Amethyst blew a kiss, went out and ran lightly up the staircase.

One of the three small bedrooms had already been transformed into a nursery. There were carved and painted animals set out on the broad sill and a curtain patterned with red poppies hung across the wall. The cradle in which Harcourt had been briefly rocked was at the foot of the bed in the main bedchamber, but there was a narrow bed here for the nursemaid who had been engaged for when the babe had been born, and a chest of drawers held rosemary-scented garments lovingly stitched and knitted over the past months. Myfi shuffled out of the end bedroom and greeted Amethyst with the familiarity of a long-time servant.

"So you're here again, Missy? You get prettier every time I see you!"

"Flatterer!" Amethyst bent to kiss the other's cheek. "And you, at your age, should not be cleaning bedchambers!"

"Don't try telling me that I'm too old for my work," the old woman said sharply. "I've told the mistress again and again I'm still capable of spotting a few specks of dust and sweeping them up, and I don't intend to have a younger girl brought in over my head! Now, what brings you here? Time was when we never saw you for months on end and now you are never off the doorstep!"

"I am anxious about my mother. She doesn't seem as well as usual to me," Amethyst said.

"Ah, well! it's hard for her to be carrying another child at her age," Myfi said. "She's had a stomach-ache or two recently, but nothing more than that! It's not like you to fret about someone else, mistress."

"What a character you give me!" the girl said, laughing. "I must be on my way back to Foster Farm! The evenings are drawing in fast."

"Aye! the cold season's coming," Myfi agreed, watching as Amethyst made her way back along the gallery.

The girl had had her pretty nose put out of joint by her mother's marriage, the servant reflected, but she had shown surprisingly little resentment. Odd, when one remembered how she had been reared so strictly within the confines of Pen Tân with every reason to suppose that one day the property would pass to her. Myfi shook her head and, picking up brush and dustpan, went into the nursery. It would be good to have another babe in the house. There had been too many empty years and the death of Harcourt had been a sad affair. Myfi thought that there was too much tragedy embedded in the stones of the ancient house.

"I'm just going." Amethyst put her head in at the parlour door and spoke cheerfully.

Isobel was leaning forward in her chair, hands clasped over her stomach, a faint film of perspiration on her brow.

"Are you not feeling well?" The girl spoke anxiously.

"A touch of stomach-ache. I've had it once or twice recently. It's nothing to worry about," Isobel said wanly.

"Shall I get you something?"

"No, no, dear. If you meet Jan ask him to hurry. It always comforts me to have him by – but don't alarm him. 'Tis only a slight indisposition," Isobel said, trying to smile but wincing as the pain gripped her again.

"So long as you're all right." Amethyst went out briskly to the yard and mounted up.

There was a decided snap in the air. Winter trod hard upon the heels of autumn and, even as she raised her head, a few flakes of snow were borne towards her. The sheep would soon be brought down to the lower meadows and the grain was already piled in the barns.

She spotted a figure in the distance and rode towards him, her voice cordial as she said,

"Good-day to you, Will! Isn't it cold!"

"Very cold, mistress." He spoke formally, checking his mare in her stride, though from the look on his face she guessed he would have preferred to ride on.

"What happened to Amethyst?" she enquired lightly.

"Amethyst, then." His black-lashed grey eyes were hostile. He had not yet forgiven her for making a fool of him.

"I've seen little of you these past months," she said.

"I've my work to do," he said stolidly, "and I'm betrothed."

"Betrothed?" Amethyst stared at him in disbelief.

"To Tom Price's girl. Mair and I have been walking out since Harvest."

"Tom Price the shepherd?"

"The same. He's a good man, works hard and has put a bit by for his daughter's dowry, and Mair is a good girl, strong and healthy."

Amethyst relaxed a little. It was unflattering to have Will running after another girl so soon after she herself had rejected him, but it was clear from the way he spoke that he was not in love with Mair Price. The marriage would be no real threat to her own dominion.

"I wish you well!" she said heartily, leaning from the saddle to clasp his hand. "I shall dance at your wedding with a good heart."

"Thank you." There was relief in his expression but he withdrew his own hand quickly. Amethyst, nodding him a pleasant good-day, felt a small surge of triumph. Will Bohanna might very well marry Mair Price but he would always be bound to herself.

She rode on over the high spur of land that formed a natural barrier between the two valleys and drew rein again. as she saw Jan trotting towards her, evidently on his way back from the mill. He pulled off his hat but there was a coldness in his greeting that made her want to weep.

"I have been talking to Will Bohanna," she said brightly, dismounting and looking up at him.

"Oh? Did he have anything particular to say?" Jan, too, dismounted, but his voice expressed nothing more than polite indifference.

"He tells me that he is betrothed to Tom Price's daughter."

"I heard he was walking out with her. She will make him a good wife. Marriage settles a man," Jan commented.

Amethyst, looking at him, thought that marriage could diminish a man too. He seemed tired and drained, his hair lying lank about his neck, his eyes shadowed. It was Isobel who had caused him to look like this! A man needed a young and lively wife, not an ageing one far gone in pregnancy.

"Ought there not to be pleasure in life too?" she said lightly.

"Certainly! We shall all dance at Will Bohanna's wedding. Did he say when it was to be?"

"When spring comes, I suppose. I didn't ask."

"And there's the winter to get through first." He looked suddenly so weary that she longed to throw her arms about him and hold him tightly.

"Will you come in for some refreshment?" she asked.

"I'll not turn back," he said. "I ought to be getting back. Everything is running smoothly at the mill but with prices rising it might be a good idea to raise the wages too."

"I see no reason," she said, frowning slightly.

"If it's a harsh winter the men's families will suffer."

"Let them work overtime."

"There will be no new fleeces until spring shearing and little chance for the men to work extra."

"Then the mill itself will lose money," she said. "I doubt if you will starve," he said dryly.

She could not bear that he should think her ungenerous and so cried impulsively,

"Raise all the wages by a shilling a week, then."

"The men will be pleased," he said, the harsh lines of his face softening.

"I've no wish to see them suffer," she said demurely.

"And I must ride on. You've been up to 'Rowan Garth'?"

"For an hour. My mother seems unwell to me, but she told me that I fret too much, and that women are often thus before their babes are born."

"Your mother is probably right. She knows more about these things than I do," Jan said. "It is sometimes a hard thing for a woman to carry a child."

He sounded dispirited as if Isobel's various discomforts had affected him too. At least he would not be sleeping with her at this time. To prevent that, Amethyst would have been willing to see her mother in a permanent state of pregnancy.

"You look troubled." She spoke gently and, looking up, saw the beginning of desire in his eyes. A moment more and he would take her in his arms. He stepped back, his voice curt as he said,

"I must get back to Isobel. I will tell the men about the increase in their wages and make sure they know it is due to you."

She could not have cared less about the men and their wages, but she nodded, watching him mount up again and ride off. It had not been possible to delay him any further with exciting his suspicion. By now surely the pains would be too far advanced for much to be done. She took Cariad's rein and went on foot down the sloping track, her head high as she walked along. Soon, very soon, Jan would turn to her, needing comfort, and out of his need she would kindle desire. He had felt it for her once and crushed it down but it could be nursed into life again. She was as sure of that as she was of her own beauty.

Mistress Jenkins and she sat later at each side of a glowing fire, the housekeeper with her knitting, Amethyst staring into the leaping flames. Flames such as Cassian, her true father, would now be suffering in. She wondered if what the Reverend Elias said was true, if the wicked truly writhed in hell-fire for all eternity. Eternity was a word that spread itself far beyond the limits of her understanding. She preferred to leave such words for the Reverend Elias to ponder.

"Horseman riding past," Mistress Jenkins said, raising her head from her work.

"Riding fast too. I wonder what's amiss?" Amethyst rose and went over to the window, opening it and leaning to listen. The hoofbeats were dying into the distance but the wind was growing stronger and more snow blew into her face.

"I hope your mother is not taken bad," Mistress Jenkins said.

"Oh, so do I!" Amethyst spoke fervently, her blue eyes intense as she latched the window and came back to her companion. "She really did not look very well when I saw her this afternoon."

"We must hope all will be well," Mistress Jenkins said. "Mistress Isobel is so charming. Such an ideal marriage! I shall hope all goes well with this babe."

"We shall both pray," Amethyst said, staring into the fire.

Her mother was a good woman for all that she had lain once with her own brother. There would be no fiery hell for Isobel, only a cool, white heaven for her and her babes. Well, she was welcome to it, provided that Amethyst could have Jan. Her longing for him had grown stronger during the months of frustration.

"I saw Will Bohanna," she said. "He and Mair Price are betrothed."

"Are they so? Oh, she's a fine wench," Mistress Jenkins said, effectively diverted. "She hasn't much in the way of dowry, mind, but Will Bohanna has a solid future. Not many men of his age have such a position."

"He is a good steward, so my mother says," Amethyst said coolly. "I shall look forward to going to the wedding."

"And one day we shall be dancing at your own wedding," Mistress Jenkins said.

"Oh, I don't believe that I will ever marry," Amethyst smiled. "You and I will live together like peas in a pod until we are old ladies."

The idea evidently tickled the housekeeper's fancy, for she giggled appreciatively as she deftly turned the heel on the stocking she was making, and her worries about the passing horseman evidently went out of her mind. If any other riders passed Foster Farm that night the increasing snow muffled their hoofbeats and Amethyst herself slept more soundly than she had slept for ages.

A thunderous hammering on the door woke her just before dawn. She groped in the half light for her slippers, pulled on a warm robe and padded down the stairs. As she drew the bolts she was already composing her face to receive bad tidings.

"Jan! What brings you here so early?"

She broke off for he had thrust his way past her into the kitchen, not troubling to scrape the snow from his boots. She closed the door and moved to the windows, unfolding the wooden shutters upon a grey, white-flecked world. The half light revealed the warm ashes of the hearth, his own white face and heavy eyes.

"Something is amiss," she said, surprised at the nervousness that flooded through her.

"And you are the one to explain it," he said tightly.

"Explain what? I cannot tell what you mean," she began. "Pennyroyal," he interrupted. "In God's name what possessed you to put pennyroyal in your mother's drink?"

She opened her mouth to reply but he went on harshly, his accusing eyes never leaving her face.

"It's no use your denying it! Myfi tasted the dregs of your mother's drink and recognised the taste. She found Isobel doubled up with pain and feared poison. Not deliberate, for her mind does not run along those lines, but an accidental thing. What possessed you?"

"Mistress Gerthe mentioned that women in childbirth sometimes had recourse to pennyroyal."

"As an aid to abortion! You must have heard her say that too."

"If ever she did I don't recall it," Amethyst said quickly. "Pennyroyal for childbirth is what I remember her saying. Perhaps she was confused. You know how forgetful she became just before the end. My mother has been looking so unwell that I thought a pinch of pennyroyal might help. I never meant to cause any harm."

"You had no right to put any herb or physic into Isobel's drink," he said angrily. "Since when were you licensed as an apothecary? Since when was your medical advice sought?"

"I only wanted to help." She began to cry gently, letting the tears slide down her face. "I was anxious about my mother and I thought the pennyroyal would make her feel better. I ought to have asked leave but I never did. Blame me for that but not for anything else, for I meant no harm."

"God knows I'd like to believe so," he muttered, staring down at her.

"I can scarce tell one herb from another," she said pitifully, "but the jars are labelled, and I remember Mistress Gerthe speaking of pennyroyal. Oh, but it's a hard matter to try to help and be so stupid as I am!"

So stupid that I forgot to rinse out the tankards.

"In future you'll not meddle with those herbs unless you ask leave," he said sternly.

"I will burn them!" she cried. "I will make a grand bonfire and be rid of them all!"

"Herbs have their uses and there's no sense in waste," he frowned. "But you must learn not to meddle. You almost caused a great tragedy."

"Almost! You mean my mother is not – ?" Amethyst stared at him.

"She seemed a little better for a while," Jan said, "and then the pains began again. I sent Will Bohanna for the physician but before they returned Isobel was delivered of a boy. Praise be that she stood the ordeal so well. I sat with her the whole night through and she has slept deeply and shows no sign of fever. I must get back to her."

"But not while you are still angry with me." She caught at his arm, tears sparkling on her cheeks. "I cannot bear it when you are angry with me! As it is I shall never forgive myself! My mother – was she angry too?"

"She knows nothing about the pennyroyal. Nobody knows save Myfi and I told her it was clearly an accident and that no good ever came of gossip. It was an accident, wasn't it?"

His tone begged for reassurance.

"It tears my heart that you should doubt it," she said forlornly.

"It is only that I am bone-weary and confused. I had no reason to suppose – "

"This has been a bad year," she said gently. "First, your poor babe and then your mother and now – "

"God is good," he said gravely. "Your mother took small hurt and there is hope for the babe."

"The babe lived?"

"A seven-month babe sometimes does and he is quite perfect. Tiny but perfect. We are calling him Lowell. It's a name Isobel likes, though I cannot pretend to care for it myself, but I think I'd give her the world now out of sheer gratitude for her safe delivery!"

"Lowell Schneider."

"Future master of Pen Tân, though he's no more than a scrap of flesh and blood now. We will have him baptised in the house in a day or two. Will you come?"

"If you are still not angry with me," she said tremulously.

"I am not angry, but you must leave physic to those who understand its effects."

"I'll never use herbs again unless I know exactly what I'm doing," she promised.

"Best not to use them at all. We cannot have you poisoning the entire neighbourhood. I'll be getting back. Pray for your new brother. He was born safely but he's very tiny and winter is here." He pinched her cheek, the anger vanished from his expression, and turned to go.

She made no move to delay him. There was no point. At this moment his mind and heart were at 'Rowan Garth' with his wife and son, and it was only the merest chance and his own fundamental inability to recognise evil intent that had saved her from an accusation of worse than meddling.

She went over to the fire and stared into the grey ashes of the burnt-out logs. There was still a faint flicker of red there but it was too early to rekindle it yet.

# Seven

The wedding of Will Bohanna to Mair Price had been an eagerly anticipated event. It was something to look forward to after the harsh winter and the slow thaw, a time to relax and enjoy good fellowship in the happy certainty that the spring planting and shearing were accomplished and the tips of the corn already green above the brown furrows. The mill had been closed for the day and a picnic luncheon spread out in the meadow outside the walls of 'Rowan Garth'. The only risk was the weather but it had begun fine and promised to continue fair.

Amethyst had breakfasted early and now, mounted on Cariad, rode up the narrow path that wound past the church to the Price cottage. Tom Price was already making the rounds of his charges, his bitch Ceri at his heels, for not even his only daughter's wedding day could divert him from his duties, but Mair was within. Her plump form flitted past the small window as Amethyst dismounted and, a moment later, she appeared on the threshold, an expression of not entirely welcoming surprise on her face.

Mair had never exchanged more than a Sunday greeting with Amethyst Prester and was privately of the opinion that the other was a stuck-up piece with little to be stuck up about. She had certainly never visited the cottage before and Mair was not overjoyed to see her there now.

"Good morrow, Mair!" Her voice and smile were cordial. "Not cleaning today, surely? You should be making yourself beautiful!"

"I like to leave the place decent for my dad," Mair said, but she could not check a quick downward glance at her work-roughened hands.

"He will miss you but that's a fate all parents must suffer," Amethyst said, tugging a bundle out of the saddlebag. "I don't live with my mother."

"But you are not wed," Mair pointed out.

"No, indeed!" Amethyst agreed. "I don't have to catch a husband before I set up as an independent lady. You will be moving into quite a crowded household. Will has five sisters, hasn't he? And none of them wed?"

"I will enjoy the company," Mair said.

"Indeed it must get lonely when your father is out with the sheep all day," Amethyst sympathised. "Are you going to invite me in?"

"Yes. Yes, of course." Mair stood hastily aside, allowing the taller girl to precede her into the cottage. At least the room that served as general living quarters was spotlessly clean, the floor swept and scattered with new rushes, the fire built up, the stools and tables set back against the walls. She had baked bread the previous day and prepared a casserole that would serve her father for a couple of days if he reheated it. She could come over two or three times a week in order to check on his welfare.

"Such a small room," Amethyst remarked, glancing

round. "I see that I was wrong. Far from being crowded out in the Bohanna house you will have more space than you know how to occupy!"

"Can I do something for you?" Mair interrupted. "I wanted to make myself ready."

"Which is exactly why I came!" Amethyst held out the bundle. "I hope I've gauged your size aright."

"It's a gown," Mair said blankly.

"I hope you will wear it today," Amethyst said.

"Well, I had made … " The girl bit her lip.

"Wear this. It is the latest fashion at Court, they say. I wanted to give you a present."

"I'm sure it's very kind of you," Mair said, the doubt in her eyes turning to brightness as she held up the pink taffeta with its panels of embroidered lace. "I never had such a beautiful dress before in all my life."

"Wear it, then." Amethyst smiled and took another glance about the room. "After all, you are marrying a man who has a considerable position. You will be wife to the steward of Pen Tân. Oh, for myself it would not have been a suitable match but for the daughter of a steward – "

"For yourself, mistress?"

"Oh, it would not have done at all," Amethyst said earnestly. "It was my own fault for showing friendship to him, of course. It never entered my head that he might take it as encouragement to something more. I fear I hurt him. But then he turned to you and I was so relieved to know that he had settled on a wife more suitable to his estate. You will make him very happy, my dear Mair. Very happy."

"You and Will?" Mair was staring at her, distress in her round, freckled face.

"Indeed not! It was never anything but friendship," Amethyst said. "I told him frankly that anything more was impossible. Out of the question! I felt guilty, thinking I might have led him to expect more. Will is so romantic but you don't need me to tell you that!"

"No, indeed," Mair said, her voice still blank.

"And so you must wear the gown as a token of my good wishes for your future happiness," Amethyst said.

"It's very kind of you." Some of the brightness returned to the girl's eyes as she fingered the taffeta.

"In that gown Will will forget that I ever existed," Amethyst murmured as she went out to Cariad again.

Mair stayed where she was, smoothing the bright pink folds, but trouble was mingled with the brightness in her face, and she didn't respond to Amethyst's parting wave as the girl trotted away down the hill.

The morning had begun well, she considered. Will Bohanna would soon learn that he had acted discourteously in turning to another wench so soon after she had rejected him!

The church was crowded and there were flowers to decorate the communion table. With King Charles upon the throne much of the old beauty of ritual was creeping back. Jan was not sure if he approved or not, but when his glance strayed to Isobel his eyes were warmly appreciative. She had recovered from the ordeal of childbirth more quickly than he had dared to hope and, in her warm gown of apricot velvet, looked charming. Her fair hair was not yet touched with grey and the colour in her cheeks owed nothing to rouge. Lowell was at home in the care of the two maids but he was a fine baby, light and small but very healthy. Isobel was suckling him herself and nothing delighted him more than to watch the two of them together, she baring her white breast for the seeking mouth.

His glance shifted to where Amethyst sat. She wore a gown of creamy wool, high-necked and full-sleeved, its wide skirts finely pleated, its hem thickly embroidered with dark green leaves. Her face was pale but her curls glowed as brightly as rowan berries in the shaft of sunlight that came through the window. She was near seventeen and disturbingly attractive. A husband would have to be found for her soon but it would have to be a man worthy of her, a man capable of controlling her strong will and wayward passions.

The bridegroom wore what was obviously his best suit of clothes, and had sleeked down his black, curly hair. He looked intensely nervous, his fingers twisting his hat round and round, the toe of one shoe furtively rubbing against the back of his other leg. The fiddler was striking up the wedding march, and there was a general craning of necks as the bride entered.

'A good-looking girl, Jan thought. Respectable and healthy. It was a pity she had chosen such an unsuitable gown. The dress was too bright a shade for her red cheeks and too low in the neck for one of her station. Will had given her a faintly startled glance as she reached his side. She clutched a bouquet of yellow roses and her veil was pinned to her head with another yellow rose.

She looks like a large pink pig in that dress, Amethyst thought happily. Will always had good taste, good taste for a steward, that is. He will learn to regret his lack of fidelity. She lowered her eyes to the prayer book in her hand, her profile madonna pure in the spring sunshine.

The marriage was accomplished. Will had put a gold ring on Mair's roughened finger and kissed her briefly on the cheek, and they were all coming out into the churchyard, the children jumping up and down in wild excitement as the bridegroom flung sweetmeats for them from a pouch he carried. A cart decorated with greenery stood ready to take the newly-weds to the marriage feast and the guests were mounting their own ponies and beginning to ride up the track.

"A most auspicious day!" Master Elias said chattily.

"Indeed it is!" Amethyst perched sidesaddle on Cariad, smiled down at the minister.

"And perhaps we shall have the joy of your own nuptials before too long," he hinted.

"That isn't very likely. I fear that I am born to be an old maid," she answered jestingly and spurred after the long cavalcade winding over the hill.

An awning had been erected for fear of sudden change in the weather, but the sky was cloudless and the long tables groaned with a variety of pies, cold meats, jellies and sweetmeats. The bride and groom stood within the awning, formally greeting people they saw nearly every day.

"Mair, how grand you look!" Amethyst, Cariad's reins looped over her arm, went smilingly to shake the bride's hand.

"Thank you, mistress." Mair answered politely but her expression was cool. Amethyst wondered if the foolish wench had begun to realise how unsuitable the dress was.

"Will!" She moved on to the bridegroom. "What a fortunate man you are, to be sure. Allow me to wish you every happiness."

"That's very kind of you." His eyes flicked over her slender cream-sheathed figure. She hoped she could discern regret in his gaze.

"You have chosen a fine, healthy wench. She will give you many children, I don't doubt," Amethyst purred.

"We hope so, mistress," he answered stolidly, the blush in his cheeks deepening.

He was really rather stupid after all, she thought, leading Cariad across the bright grass to the stableyard.

The main door stood open and, having stabled Cariad, she slipped within. The hall was empty and when she called softly up the stairs nobody responded. No doubt the servants had joined the wedding reception, carrying little Master Lowell with them. For a brief space of time she had the house she loved entirely to herself.

She stood, gazing around the wide chamber, her face gentle. This house soothed her fiery spirit and quenched for a little time the restless yearning within her. It was simply not possible that she would never be mistress here. God would not be so unkind as to deny her her rights in blood. Some happy accident would – must befall the babe, and Isobel must never again conceive. For the moment, however, there was leisure to stand, to let the peace of the old building soak into her bones.

There was a hesitant footfall behind her and she swung about, one hand at her throat, her wide eyes on the slender young man who confronted her. Gracefully built, with dark travelling clothes contrasting with light skin and hair, he looked as startled as she but recovered himself more rapidly.

"Mistress, my apologies for startling you! Master Aubrey

Clare, at your service. I was bidden by the servant to wait here."

"Amethyst Prester," she said automatically. "To wait for whom?"

"For Master Schneider. I rode here at his invitation."

"Oh?" She studied him curiously, her head tilted.

"I am here on business. My father is a merchant with interests in the woollen trade. I come from Chester."

"I believe Jan mentioned the name," she said, wrinkling her brow. She took little interest in the mill apart from the steadily accumulating profits.

"I was told to wait," he repeated.

"Have you had some refreshment?" She remembered her manners in time.

"The servant left me wine and some cake. She mentioned a wedding so I fear I come at an inconvenient time."

"Not in the least. Our steward is marrying a local girl. We will join the guests later, but tell me about yourself first."

She led the way back into the parlour and seated herself, aware of his admiring eyes as the sunlight caught her in its beam.

"Do sit down. Master Schneider is sure to come in soon and if he does not then we will seek him together," she invited.

"Thank you, Mistress Prester?" There was a faint question in his voice.

"I am Master Schneider's daughter," she explained, "but I took my mother's maiden name as I was born before their marriage."

She was amused to see the colour run up under his fair skin. Although he was evidently in his twenties there was nothing sophisticated about him.

"I am also the owner of Foster Farm, that is where the mill is built," she continued.

"I believe I rode past on the way here. Master Schneider manages it for you, then?"

"He was a weaver in his native Flanders," she explained. "For my own part I know very little about the woollen business, but I suppose you are an expert."

"On the contrary. I merely work for my father," he said. "He has been in poor health recently and so my brother and I have taken a larger share of the responsibilities. Charles is wed and his wife with child so he has elected to cut down his travelling until after the babe is born, and I undertake most of the journeying."

"Your wife, I take it, is not with child?"

With amusement she noticed the blush flare into his face again.

"I have no wife," he said. "I was always somewhat shy with the ladies."

"A recommendation. Most gentlemen are overbold," she said pleasantly. "You will be staying at 'Rowan Garth' for a few days, I hope?"

"Master Schneider did invite me to stay for a week or two. Did he not mention it?"

"He probably did, but we have been so occupied with preparations for this wedding that it must have slipped my mind."

"Young ladies are generally more interested in weddings than in business," he said, with the air of one uttering a great wisdom.

"True, but it is a sad reflection on my own abilities. I

hope you will dine with me at Foster Farm."

"You don't live here, then?" He looked surprised.

"Our situation is an unusual one," Amethyst said. "Foster Farm was willed to me by my grandmother and, as my parents, being newly wed, had a very natural desire to be alone. I was sent to live on my own property. It is a pleasant house and I have an excellent chaperon, but I cannot forbear from thinking of this place as home."

"It is natural," he nodded.

"Of course I am made most welcome and invited to visit often." She moved her hands gently and let her voice trail into a regretful silence.

"It must be lonely," Aubrey Clare said with sympathy.

"One grows accustomed to loneliness," she murmured. "But I confess that I have longed to travel. It must be so exciting to visit a great city. Have you ever been to London?"

"Twice," he said. "My father took both Charles and me to London some years ago, before his health failed. We took lodgings near St Paul's. There was much rebuilding being carried out after the great fire but it was still a fine city. We went to the play and watched the bear-baiting and a cockfight – but they would be too rough for ladies! You would like better the water pageants on the Thames and the gardens at Chelsea. One can milk one's own cow there and pick strawberries when they are in season."

Amethyst privately thought that Londoners must be completely mad to go milking cows for pleasure but she smiled encouragingly.

"Did you see the King? They say he is very attractive to the ladies."

"And they to him! We saw him riding to some fête or other. Very tall with a curly black wig and an ugly mouth, but ready to speak to all. We could not get near enough in the crowd for that but we saw him clearly."

"Were you in London for a long time?"

"More than a month. Of course my father had business acquaintances to see."

"His interests are wide, then?"

"Mainly textiles. A little silver and copper too, and spices. He is part owner of a vessel that trades with the East," Aubrey Clare said proudly.

"I am surprised you live still in Chester," she commented.

"My father says that in London he would be a merchant among merchants. In Chester he is a prince among merchants."

"I would dearly love to visit Chester."

"Oh, it's a beautiful place." He spoke soberly but his eyes shone. "There are wonderful remains of the Roman occupation there. The Romans called it Deva, as you probably know."

Amethyst, who didn't, nodded intelligently.

"One can walk along the ramparts and imagine the centurions pacing and the light from the campfires below striking on their helmets and spears. They have unearthed cooking pots and votive offerings and coins with the Emperor's head upon them. The past is all around us, side by side with the present, for it is a most prosperous town."

"It sounds fascinating," she breathed, blue eyes glowing as they fixed on his face. "You should have been an historian."

"I would have liked it above all things," he confided,

"but my father wished his two sons to follow him in business. Since my mother died his whole life has been bound up in his merchant activities. Neither Charles nor I would wish to disappoint him, especially now that his health is so poor."

"What ails him?" she enquired.

"He had a bad fall from his horse some months ago and the physicians suspect an internal injury. His heart is not strong, I fear."

"It must be worrying for you," she said gently.

"More worrying for him. He was always an active man and it frets him to be confined to a chair."

"And you are very fond of him."

"That, too, is natural between father and son, especially when the father is such a good man. I would like you to meet him, Mistress Prester."

"Amethyst," she corrected. "Do use my Christian name."

"It is a most unusual one," he commented.

"My grandmother chose it, to match my eyes."

"Your eyes are brighter," he said, and blushed fiery red again.

"It is the mixture of blood, I suppose. I have Welsh, English, Spanish, even a dash of Romany in my veins."

"And Flemish," he said.

"Flem – ? Oh, Flemish too. I am a kind of mongrel, I fear, but I am comforted by my royal descent."

"Royal?"

She had put her finger unerringly on the touch of snobbery in his nature, and his voice was eager as he leaned forward.

"One of my ancestors was a love-child of Sir Jasper

Tudor, uncle to King Henry the Seventh," she said. "This serpent ring I wear was given by Sir Jasper to his love. There was even talk of a secret marriage but no proof."

"Royal blood is still royal blood," he said.

"And judging from the tales we hear there are many children who will be able to claim the same when this king is gone."

"And the poor queen a barren lady. Many a man would have put her away and taken a more fruitful wife, but King Charles is a kindly husband."

"Kindly but not faithful," she dimpled. "I would have my husband both, when he comes."

"You are not promised?"

"My parents say that I may make my own choice of mate. I will not wed until I am sure there is true affection on both sides, but there is time yet. I am not seventeen until June."

"I did not wish to imply – " he began in embarrassment.

"Nor did I take it as such," she said. "Will you have some more wine?"

"Thank you, no. I ought to make my presence known to Master Schneider, unless the servants – "

"They will probably have forgotten you're here by now," she said wryly.

"And I am keeping you from the company of your friends," he said, as a burst of laughter came through the open window. "The truth is I do not often talk so freely. By nature I am somewhat shy in the company of ladies."

"I find your talk so interesting that I forget my own manners," she said laughing and holding out her hand.

"Come! we'll go and find Master Schneider for you. I hope you stay here for several days, Master Clare. It is a change for me to have company of my own station."

"Aubrey, if you please." He smiled at her and she thought he was one of the most attractive young men she had ever seen, though his fine-drawn delicate looks were not much to her personal taste.

The reception was in full swing. The first person she saw was Will, wedding suit somewhat crumpled, dancing in the kissing-ring. His bride had laid aside veil and bouquet and was being swung from one giggling lad to the next. At the long table Master Elias was trying to do justice to the ample victuals and keep an eye on the proceedings lest they grow too indecorous.

"Will!" Her hand sliding through the crook of Aubrey Clare's arm, Amethyst raised her voice imperiously. "Will, have you seen Master Schneider?"

"He's with Mistress Isobel," Will answered, pausing in the dancing and coming towards her.

"Master Aubrey, this is my mother's steward, Will Bohanna," Amethyst said.

"The bridegroom! My congratulations." The young man shook hands cordially.

"Master Clare!" Jan was hailing them from the shadow of the awning. As usual, whenever he appeared, other men shrank. His hair was ruffled, his colour high and it was clear he was in an excellent humour.

"I come at an inconvenient time," Aubrey said, bowing politely. "I had no idea you would be occupied, but your daughter has been entertaining me most pleasantly."

"I am delighted to see you again," Jan said. "Amethyst, I became acquainted with Master Clare when I visited Chester last year. His father is interested in buying our cloth."

"He told me." Amethyst tried to put reproach into her voice, but she could not. Even standing near to Jan made her feel weak and warm, unable to stand on her dignity as owner of Foster Farm.

"My – daughter takes little interest in the weaving of cloth," Jan said. "But this is a celebration. We can defer any talk of business until tomorrow."

"Come and meet my mother." Amethyst interrupted, her grip firm on Aubrey Clare's arm, her blue eyes sparkling.

For the first time in her life she faced Jan with a personable young man at her side. She looked hopefully for some sign of jealousy, but Jan smiled, clapping the visitor on the shoulder.

"Enjoy yourself, Master Clare. Is your baggage at the house?"

"Your servant took it up. She did say that she would inform you."

"Myfi has nothing in her head at the moment beyond cakes and ale," Amethyst said.

"I'd best make sure that my son and heir is in good hands, then," Jan said. "We'll talk later, Master Clare. I trust your father is in good health?"

"As good as it ever is, sir."

As Jan bowed again and hurried away, the young man said, "I was under the impression that the babe had died."

"The first one did. That was Harcourt. I have a new little brother now," Amethyst said. "Lowell is the apple of our eyes, though he was born prematurely. Indeed, we greatly feared for his life because he was so tiny, but he is thriving now. I positively dote on him."

Aubrey Clare, glancing at her, thought he had never seen a girl with a sweeter face.

# *Eight*

Her trunk was packed, the rest of her belongings stowed away in the saddlebags. Amethyst, adjusting her hat before the mirror, felt a trifle amused at the speed with which events had occurred. Or perhaps it would be more true to say that she had caused events to happen more quickly that she could have dared to hope.

Master Aubrey Clare improved on acquaintance, though she had been prepared to find her first impression erroneous, but he was proving to be a charming companion. Much of his day was spent, out of necessity, discussing business with Jan, but he was always ready to chat with her when the more serious part of the day was done, and in the days following his arrival she looked forward to seeing him ride up the gate of Foster Farm with an expectant smile on his pleasant face.

Sometimes they merely sat in the parlour, under Mistress Jenkin's indulgent eye and he told her about his home in Chester, painting his life so vividly that she could almost smell the pungent scent of his father's tobacco, feel the rough velvet of the peaches growing against the south wall.

The Clares had been merchants for generations, building

up a solid fortune and an equally solid reputation through a mixture of shrewdness and honesty. They had made sound, if unspectacular, marriages and by being carefully moderate in politics and religion had kept away from the attention of the authorities. They were respectable people with the occasional emergence of an artistic son or daughter to leaven the dullness.

"One of my ancestors actually set out on a Crusade," Aubrey said. "He didn't get farther than Calais, where he expired of the sweating sickness, but his intention must have counted for something!"

He had watched her with pleasure as she laughed. When Amethyst was amused her eyes were warm and her small white teeth bit down upon her underlip. Amethyst, fully aware of the effect she was creating, took care to laugh a lot when Aubrey Clare was with her.

They rode together too, she in her blue riding-habit with a feather to soften the bright hue of her curls, he in his dark travelling-dress, his fair head bent towards her, his own laughter ringing out when she told him amusing, invented tales of the neighbours. Mistress Jenkins, fortunately, regarded horses as a speedy but uncomfortable way of getting from one place to another, and preferred to stay at home.

What was becoming increasingly obvious was that Aubrey Clare had concluded his business, but still lingered on at 'Rowan Garth'.

"The young man seems to have taken up permanent residence with us," Jan remarked to Isobel.

"He spends most of his time with Amethyst, so we are not faced with the problem of entertaining him," Isobel said reasonably.

"But his father is bound to call him home soon. From what I know of Richard Clare he is not the type to let his sons run idle."

"Perhaps he has other business in mind," Isobel said.

"We've signed contracts for the wool."

"I meant Amethyst. It's plain that he admires her greatly. I suspect that he is considering making an offer for her hand."

"She is too young," Jan said.

"She will be seventeen in less than two months!"

"Young for her years I meant. Don't thrust her too quickly out of childhood."

Isobel, looking at him with a heart-clutching insight, thought that even Jan was not aware of the reality that lay behind his words. The truth was that he had no desire to see Amethyst in the arms of any other man, and the pity of it was that if she ever tried to explain it to him he would find it impossible to believe. Abruptly she said, with an air of changing the conversation,

"I believe I am with child again."

"So soon? I thought women could not conceive while they were suckling!"

"It seems that I am an exception to the rule," she said dryly.

"Do you feel well?" Amethyst banished from his mind, he came over and took Isobel's hand.

"I feel marvellous," she said truthfully.

"This one will be a daughter," he said. "I would give much for a little daughter."

He would never learn to think of Amethyst as his own child. Smiling at him she resolved to encourage Aubrey Clare to stay as long as possible.

The subject of their discussion was at that moment wreathing daisies and cornflowers into a garland. They had dismounted and she was seated on a grassy knoll, blossoms piled in her lap, while Aubrey sat at a little distance, watching her.

"Can one do this in a city?" she asked playfully.

"Ride a little way beyond the walls and you may sit in fields as green as this."

"But with no mountains in the distance," she said with a touch of wistfulness.

"If you came to Chester I could show you sights to compare with this," he said eagerly. "You did tell me that you would like to travel!"

"I would, but females cannot just pack their bags and wander at will," she protested.

"If we were wed – " He broke off his fair skin reddening.

"Wed?" She sat very still, the flowers dripping petals from her fingers.

"I meant to lead up to this very slowly in the proper manner," he said, rising and dropping to his knee at her side. "The truth is that I never felt so much at ease with a young lady in my life before as I feel with you. I intended to speak to Master Schneider first and to talk to my own father, though I guarantee that he will make no objection. Instead, I make a fool of myself and blurt it out."

"You want me to marry you, after knowing me for so short a space of time?" she asked.

"I don't think time has anything to do with it," Aubrey said. "I shall never love you more than I do at this moment, Mistress Amethyst. I shall never love any woman as I love you. The first moment I saw you I felt as if I knew you, had always known you."

"I have enjoyed your company," she murmured, lowering her eyes modestly. Under the high, frilled collar of her bodice a pulse in her throat beat fast.

"No more than that? I hoped – it may have been presumptuous of me – but I hoped you might have begun to feel something more."

"I cannot tell what I feel," she said, making a helpless little gesture with her hands. The partly made garland slithered to the grass.

"Perhaps there is another man? If so then please tell me and put me out of my suspense," he begged.

"I told you that I was not promised to anyone," she evaded.

"And you don't dislike me?"

"I told you that I enjoy your company," she said earnestly. "There are no young men here who interest me."

That at least was true. Jan was near forty and could no longer be considered young.

"Then you will consider?" His face was lit with hope, but she was conscious of a weakness in its delicate planes, an over-sensitivity about his mouth. If she married him she would certainly be allowed to have her own way.

"You will let me speak to your father?" he was persisting.

"No!" She spoke so sharply that he flinched. "No, not yet." She put her hand on his shoulder, gentling her tone. "I am not certain of my own mind. Oh, I like you well, and there is no other young man, but I have never been out of the country. Perhaps in your own place you might not seem so attractive."

"Perhaps you might see me as more attractive," he said

with a hint of humour in his tone.

"Oh, I hope that it will be so," she said softly, "but how can I tell?"

"You could visit Chester," he said.

"Visit without invitation? I hardly see – "

"I swear my father would be only too pleased to welcome a visitor," Aubrey said. "He finds life very tedious since his accident and looks forward very much indeed to company. We have a large house, only my father and myself there since my brother married."

"I cannot pay a visit to two unmarried gentlemen without a chaperon!" she exclaimed virtuously.

. "Mistress Jenkins could come with you. She would enjoy the trip?"

"She would overwhelm me with gratitude," Amethyst said dryly.

"Then won't you come? I could send word to my father to expect you and your chaperon, so that the guest-rooms could be made ready."

"I'd come as a friend," she said slowly. "I'd not want you to think that my visit was a prelude to our marriage. I'd not want to raise false hopes."

"But if you were happy – if you found the city was your place – you might agree to wed me? You say you like me."

"I like old Peblig, the blind fiddler, but I am not about to marry him. There must be more than liking."

"On my side there is!"

"But not yet on mine. You must not rush me into a declaration I might regret!"

"You might grow into the way of loving me when you have stayed in my home for a few months."

"It's possible." Seeing his crestfallen face she amended to, "It's probable. I cannot and will not say more than that. If I visit your home it will be as a friend. I want no ties between us, spoken or unspoken, for I need time. I do need time."

"Stay until Harvest," he urged. "I'll not press you for a decision until the summer is out. I'll keep my feelings hidden and not even tell my father my hopes. Come, I cannot be fairer than that, can I?"

"Give me a few hours to decide," she said slowly.

"If you need hours simply to decide to pay a visit," he said, looking crestfallen, "then my hope is not as high as it was."

"Dear Master Aubrey." Her hand lingered on his shoulder. "You must not give up so easily, else you will never win your heart's desire! Come! cheer up, my dear friend. Remember how I like good company, and smile."

He seized her hand and kissed her fingers with a passion that might have touched her had it not betrayed a clumsiness that irritated her.

"We had better go back," she said, rising and shaking her skirt free of the remaining blossoms. "Will you call on me tomorrow and I'll tell you what I have decided?"

"Until tomorrow." His hand lingered shyly at her waist, but she untethered Cariad and mounted briskly, cantering down the hill without a second glance at the discarded garland.

To spend the summer in Chester was a tempting prospect. She had enjoyed Aubrey describing the life of the city, had thought it would be interesting to see the places of which he spoke for herself. But it would mean months away from Pen Tân, months when she would not have the bitter-sweet pleasure of seeing Jan and talking to him, months when she lived in a strange household. She was not certain she could endure that, but she had no wish to be deprived of the flattering attentions of a personable young gentleman.

She rode back to Foster Farm with her brain reeling, scarcely aware of the young man trailing after her. For the first time after one of their rides she merely waved her hand, as she went into the yard, without inviting him in for a tankard of wine. He went past slowly, turning to smile at her with a mixture of hope and trepidation in his expression that was most flattering.

"Did you enjoy your ride?" Mistress Jenkins called out as she came in from the stable.

"Very much." Amethyst spoke cheerfully.

"Master Schneider came a few moments since."

"And I missed him!" She had wasted time fooling with a love-sick young man, when she might have been enjoying Jan's company.

"He went over to the mill," the housekeeper said. She spoke into thin air, her charge having turned immediately and gone out again. The girl was restless, Mistress Jenkins thought with a sigh. For ever in and out, up and down, as if she had an imp within her. Still, she was lively and good-hearted and life was easier than it had ever been for the housekeeper. Smiling her gratitude to the empty kitchen she went over to the dresser and helped herself to a nip of sherry, raising her goblet in a silent toast to present luxury.

Jan was just emerging from the long weaving-shed and Amethyst slowed her pace as she approached, her face and voice deliberately casual.

"Good day to you! Mistress Jenkins said you'd been over

to the house. I was out riding with Master Aubrey."

"Between you, you must have covered every inch of the district," he remarked.

"Oh, I find him a charming young man. It is such a treat for me to have a companion."

"Are you so lonely, then?" He caught her up on her words, his face anxious.

"Not when you are here." She tucked her hand through his arm and glanced up at him through her lashes.

"I stand as your father," he said coldly, but his arm quivered as if her touch had wakened something within him.

"But not in blood," she said softly.

"And I love Isobel most dearly. Most dearly!" he repeated fiercely.

"Master Aubrey is beginning to have an affection for me," Amethyst said. "He wished me to pay a long visit to his home. His father would be most happy, he says, to entertain a visitor, and, naturally, Mistress Jenkins would chaperon me. It would mean closing up the house for a couple of months, but someone could go in to keep it clean and fresh, and it would be most interesting to see Chester. I have never been anywhere in my life. Of course, if you forbade it, I would give up the idea."

There was a desperate hope in her voice. If he turned now and said he could not bear to be absent from her for the summer she would give up all thought of going to Chester.

"Isobel is with child again," he said.

"Already?" Her hand withdrew from his arm as she stared at him in consternation.

"Lowell is seven months. There will be a year between him and the new babe."

So Isobel had conceived again! No doubt she would bear a child every year until she was past childbearing age! Every conception was proof that Jan had made love to her; every birth was another person to stand between herself and 'Rowan Garth'.

"Would you mind if I went on a visit to Chester?" she asked.

"If it would please you to go, but does this mean that Master Aubrey is about to ask me for your hand?" he enquired.

"Indeed not!" she said quickly. "I have made it clear that there is absolutely nothing between us except friendship. I would welcome a change, that's all. But if you don't wish me to go?"

"Oh, go by all means," he said, so promptly that it tore at her heart. "A visit to the city will do you good, my dear. Even if you are not inclined to Master Aubrey you will have the opportunity to meet other young gentlemen of good station."

"I don't wish to marry," she said, twisting her fingers together. "I never could bear to let any other man touch me. Don't you understand?"

"I think it best we don't continue in this vein," Jan said.

"But there is never opportunity to talk," she said, words spilling out of her. "Either my mother or Master Aubrey or Mistress Jenkins is always there. We are never alone."

"Even if we were, nothing would happen," he interrupted.

"So I may as well go to Chester," she said in a hurt little voice. "You will not even miss me."

"Not miss you!" They had crossed the meadow and were

near the foot of the slope leading up to the crest and he stopped dead, swinging her about to face him. There was anger in his expression, and the dawning of something else. The hope flared up in her again, and she swayed towards him, eyes shining as her lips parted.

"I love your mother," he said, and gave her a little shake. "I have loved Isobel since the first moment I saw her. Even after – after her brother dishonoured her, I went on loving her. For fifteen years I went on loving her and then you came, young and lovely, and I wanted her more intensely than ever."

"You wanted me!" she flashed. "I was the one you wanted!"

"Perhaps." He let her go, the anger dying out of his face. "A man would need to be blinded or a half-wit not to want a beautiful creature like you, but it is Isobel I love. It is Isobel I shall always love. You must make up your mind to it now and not waste all the sweetness of your youth in waiting for what can never happen."

"We are not related in blood," she said.

"But we are related in law! Any association between us would be regarded as incest, even if I had any intention of ever taking you. Lord knows I am as prone to temptation as any man, but I'll not spoil a young girl's life by betraying her, and I'll not hurt Isobel or soil our love. You had best make up your mind to it!"

"You're a hard man," she said slowly. "I never knew before how unyielding goodness could be."

"It is better so. I want you to be happy, Amethyst. There would only be shame and grief for you when the pleasure was done, and for me the pangs of remorse. I could never again look your mother in the face."

"Always my mother," she said.

"Because it is Isobel whom I love," he said simply. "It will always be Isobel, my dear."

"Then I will while away the summer in Chester," she said, her voice almost gay. "Perhaps I will even take a husband while I am there. Master Aubrey or some other young man who catches my fancy. You will not make objection, I hope?"

"I have not the right," he said sombrely.

"In law you have! In law you are my guardian and may forbid me to marry."

"Marry where you choose!" he turned and began to walk rapidly back to where his mount was tethered.

"Oh, I shall! I shall indeed!" she called after him. "I shall have a wonderful time in the city!"

She would buy some pretty gowns and some fashionable hats, she decided. She might even use a little paint on her face. Her complexion needed none, but she had heard that Court ladies wore it thickly.

Mistress Jenkins, informed that they were to travel to Chester, had needed several nips of fortifying sherry before she could adequately express her excited gratitude.

"Sam, God rest him! went to Chester once. He said that it was full of English folk, but they were very polite and friendly. And to think that I shall be going there too! Wonders never cease, do they, Mistress Amethyst! Does this mean you are betrothed to the young gentleman?"

"It means nothing of the sort," Amethyst snapped. "Master Richard Clare is a merchant and I am the owner of a mill. Isn't it natural for us to meet and discuss business?"

"I thought Master Aubrey and Master Schneider were taking care of that," the housekeeper said.

"Perhaps I intend to take a more active interest in future," Amethyst said grandly. "Anyway, I have the right to go visiting, haven't I? I don't wish to spend my entire life cooped up in the mountains."

To Isobel she gave much the same reasons, her blue eyes guileless as they fixed on her mother's face.

"I will be back in good time for the birth. A few months away will distract my mind from life's cares."

"I didn't know you had any cares," Isobel said with a hint of dryness.

"Oh, 'tis boredom mainly! When the chance comes to go visiting, I'd be foolish not to take it."

"You won't hurt that young man?" Isobel asked suddenly, her eyes anxious as she stared at her daughter. "He is a good man, Amethyst, and he admires you greatly."

"I don't intend to hurt anyone," the girl said. "I am very fond of Master Aubrey."

"And you will consider betrothal?"

"How anxious you are to have me married off!" Amethyst exclaimed laughing. "I shall come home heartfree, I dare swear! In time to welcome a new brother or sister."

Involuntarily both glanced towards the cradle where Lowell lay, swaddled and sleeping. Amethyst's eyes were full of gentle regret. The babe was thriving and likely to grow up strong and healthy, and Isobel was blooming. It was the greatest pity.

Isobel was a little ashamed of the relief that filled her at the thought of her daughter's going. It would be peaceful to have only Jan and little Lowell to worry about, to know that when he rode down to the mill there would be no bright-haired girl to run out and distract his attention. Sometimes, when they sat together in the evening, she would surprise a queer, unsettled look on his face and fear then that she was beginning to bore him though he was too kind to say so. Yes, it would be a peaceful summer when Amethyst had gone.

The hat, Amethyst decided now, was most becoming. It was of creamy lace with a narrow brim and long blue ribbons to match her gown. For the actual journey she would wear more serviceable garments that would stand up to the travelling but she wished to appear to her best advantage when she supped at 'Rowan Garth' this evening. She would be sweetly enticing and Jan would miss her more than he had realised when she had gone. Her lips curved into a smile as she took the hat off and fluffed out her red curls.

"Mistress Amethyst, there's Will Bohanna here to see you," Mistress Jenkins called up the stairs.

Amethyst took another satisfied look at herself in the glass, lifted her skirt and went with conscious grace down the stairs into the parlour. Dust-covers had been laid over the chairs and table and the hearth had been swept clean. Already the house looked unoccupied.

Will Bohanna stood by the window, looking awkward and embarrassed in the small chamber. He was a man more at ease in the open, she thought.

"What can I do for you, Will?" She shook his hand cordially.

"Is it true you are going away to Chester to be married?" he asked abruptly.

"Certainly not! I am going away on a visit," she said sharply.

"You've been seeing the English gentleman," he said.

"He's a visitor and it is polite to show courtesy to visitors."

"There's rumour you will wed him."

"Rumour lies!" she snapped, an angry flush coming into her cheeks. "And it is none of your business whom I choose to see. You are steward of Pen Tân, not my keeper. It is not your task to oversee my affairs."

"I don't mean to stop out of my place," he said, crimsoning in his turn. "I wanted to know if you were betrothed?"

"Well, I am not." Her voice softening, Amethyst said, "It was good of you to be anxious about me, Will."

"I still think of you," he said shyly. "I still remember how it was between us."

"There was nothing between us."

"I'll not believe that," he interrupted. "I felt more between us than mere friendship. You felt it too and spoke of it, even though you may deny it now."

"You are wed and may not talk to me thus," she said coldly.

"And Mair is a good wife." He spoke quickly as if his wife were being attacked.

"Then you must leave me to lead my own life," Amethyst said sweetly. "I certainly have no intention of interfering in yours."

"I wanted to be sure that you were – at least I can say Godspeed."

"I will return at Harvest," she assured him.

"It will be a long summer," he said.

"Dear Will!" She clasped his hand again, the irritation wiped from her face.

He still cared for her, she was thinking. The summer would indeed be a long one for him and for Jan, though he had not admitted so.

## Nine

From the top of the garden Amethyst could look over the wall and down the street to the gilded sign that hung over the shop. Master Clare kept his business and domestic arrangements strictly apart, and the separation between the two was symbolised for her by the narrow street that wound down to the main road. The shop itself was not a large one but it catered for wealthy folk who could afford to buy a roll of pale silk or a necklace set in silver. His various trading and shipping interests were carried on in the house itself and much of Richard Clare's day was spent in his study, interviewing his agents, poring over ledgers, writing letters.

The house was a handsome one and would have seemed grander if it had not been flanked by its neighbours. As it was, from the formal garden, the building looked ill-proportioned, too high for its width, the gargoyles over the door too elaborately carved.

Heavy velvet curtains hung at the windows, shutting out the sunlight even on the brightest day. The rooms within were richly and sombrely furnished with thick carpets to deaden the sound of footsteps, and sofas so heavily padded that one could scarcely rise once seated. There were cabinets crammed with ivories and copper and enamels, tall vases in which dyed feathers and rushes were arranged, carved and lacquered chests, shelves on which rows of books bound in leather and calfskin were ranged.

There was evidence of wealth everywhere one turned. Amethyst had quickly learned to calculate the value of the contents of the house but she had no way of knowing how far her host's business interests stretched or how much gold was stored in the locked chests padlocked to the floor in the study.

In a curious way the study was the heart and centre of the house, and the man who sat in the wheelchair radiated a vitality that stirred her to admiration.

She had expected a frail invalid, querulous and complaining in his insistence on being kept up to date with the intricacies of his business. Instead, she had been greeted by an elegant, silver-haired figure whose aristocratic features had echoed his son's, and whose handclasp had been unexpectedly vigorous.

"Mistress Amethyst, it is a real pleasure for me to welcome a visitor. We are too quiet here since Charles married and set up his own establishment. And now that we meet I understand why my son delayed his return."

"I hope my being here is not an inconvenience," she murmured, taking the chair he indicated. "The truth is, sir, that Master Aubrey painted the town in such glowing colours that I could not rest until I had visited."

"I have met Master Schneider, of course," he continued. "He manages the Foster mill, I understand?"

"He does indeed. I fear I have no head for business at all," she said.

"No reason why you should, my dear. Pretty wenches and hard business sense never did mix," he assured her. "But you maintain your own household?"

"I live at Foster Farm with my housekeeper, Mistress Jenkins. It's a very modest household, but our ways are quiet. I have spent all my life in the mountains."

"At your age a little gaiety doesn't come amiss," he said smilingly. "We have a pleasant social circle here among the merchant classes and lower gentry. Aubrey will be happy to escort you wherever you wish to go."

"To tell the truth, sir," she had responded, "I am so weary after the journey that I want nothing but to rest for a day or two."

"You must make yourself at home while you are here," Master Clare said warmly. "Come and go as you please, my dear Mistress Amethyst."

"You're very kind, sir." She let a dimple show briefly in her cheek as she rose.

"Not at all! It will do me great good to have a pretty young thing about the house," he responded gallantly.

Her bedroom was a handsome one, hung with blue tapestries and with a view of the grey-walled town below. She had felt a sense of constraint as they had ridden beneath an arch into narrow winding streets at each side of which shops and houses bulged out, but here in her room she had the illusion of space. Gazing through the window at the sky arching over the rooftops she tried not to think of the high crags of Pen Tân. It would be months before she could return, so it was useless to let memory tug at her heart.

Mistress Jenkins had been given a smaller chamber adjoining her own and both had the use of a small parlour, furnished in a lighter, more feminine style.

"My mother used it when she was alive," Aubrey said. "Much of the needlework in the house is her own work."

There was a stiffly posed, badly painted portrait of Mistress Clare hanging in the study, between tall bookcases crammed with books. The portrait gave no indication of the character of the sitter, but Amethyst had a mental image of a gentle creature patiently stitching at her tapestries while, in the study below, her husband, with matching quietness, built up a fortune. Her fingers itched a little at the thought. The love she craved might be denied her but it was possible for her to achieve wealth.

On that first evening they had eaten *en famille*, herself between the two men, the one young and eager, the other older, set in a mould that would not, she guessed, be altered by any outsider. He was a man who would enlarge his boundaries to include a stranger but would never change his ways. By him Aubrey seemed uncertain of himself, his features faintly blurred, his eyes begging her to notice him.

Instead, she exerted herself to be pleasant to Master Clare, listening with polite attention whenever he spoke, her eyes sparkling despite her weariness and the candlelight glinting on the serpent ring. She noticed Master Clare's own eyes fixed upon it and stretched her fingers for him to see it more closely.

"My ancestor gave it to my great-great – I don't know how may greats! – grandmother, sir," she said shyly. "They were never able to marry, but I have heard she was his one true love. The ring has been handed down through the family and so came to me."

"You are of an ancient line, then," he commented.

"Mere farmers, sir," she said modestly. "We have lived all our lives, generation after generation, save for brief periods, in the Welsh hills. Mind, we have Spanish blood in us and Romany too, so we are not entirely native!"

"Mistress Amethyst would grace any company, wouldn't she, Father?" Aubrey put in.

"Indeed she would!" Master Clare raised his goblet to her and she smiled, lowering her lashes.

That first evening had set the pattern for many that followed. Apart from a couple of scullery-maids, the servants were all male. Discreet, well trained, clearly devoted to the Clares, they ran the household with a smooth efficiency that attracted Mistress Jenkins's rapt admiration.

"Meals always on time, and the chafing dishes so beautifully hot! There have been new candles in my room every day since we arrived! It is living on a grand scale, is it not? My Sam – God rest his soul! – would be vastly surprised to see me in such a high-stepping place!"

"They are silent too," Amethyst hinted, but the housekeeper was happily oblivious.

"Most silent and well-behaved indeed! Servants are expected to know their place here and to keep it! We must take good note of it for when we are at home again, Mistress Amethyst."

"You can take good note of the cooking too," Amethyst advised. "The meals here are quite delicious. I shall have to take care lest I put on weight and grow too fat!"

She spoke with a certain complacency, knowing that she was one of those rare people who can eat until they near bursting without gaining a pound. Her high breasts and tiny waist were exquisite and her long legs gave her the added dignity of height. In her high-necked habits she had a demure look, spiced by her vivid curls and bright, slanting eyes, and when evening threw its cloak about the city she changed into a low-necked dress, rustling with lace, sensuously perfumed.

Town-life had its advantages, she decided, as the days of her visit lengthened into weeks. There were shops where one could buy anything from ribbons and laces to the finest jade and silver ornaments. At home there were the occasional trips down to Caernarvon and the visits of the pedlar when one needed to replenish one's supplies, but here one could step out into the streets and walk slowly along, pausing to gaze at the small paned windows where goods were laid out in tempting display.

The town was crowded with more people than she had ever seen in her life before. Some of them smelt none too clean, she decided critically, but there were many fashionable ladies in gowns that made her mouth water and gallants in the new baggy breeches and knee-length coats faced with gold braid. When she was on horseback she took great pleasure in showing her skill in the saddle for the benefit of the young gentlemen, who eyed her with flattering curiosity. Some of them were acquaintances of the Clares, and Aubrey made their introductions in a manner that amused her, for it was clear that while he was proud to be in her company he was anxious to keep her to himself.

It was equally clear that he was falling more and more deeply in love with her. His every glance told her that he considered her the loveliest girl he had ever met, and she suspected that he was stealing many working-hours in order to escort her. It was as well that Mistress Jenkins accompanied them, for that prevented his making any declaration to her of his passion, and in the evening they sat with his father until the stroke of ten signalled bedtime. She had wondered if Aubrey would come to her room when his father and Mistress Jenkins were asleep, but the young man was evidently honourable. Part of Amethyst was disappointed, for Aubrey was handsome, and yet she was in part relieved. It did not seem right for her to yield completely to any man save the one she truly loved.

She had been more than a month at the house before she met Aubrey's elder brother, Charles. He was a thinner, sharper version of Aubrey, with a perpetual frown etched between his brows that suggested a condition of settled anxiety, and when he bowed over her hand she had an impression of cold blue eyes giving her a swift, probing glance.

"Mistress Amethyst, my apologies for not coming before but my wife is not well. The warmer weather saps her strength, I fear, and she craves frosty days. For that reason she begs you to excuse her from meeting you for a little while."

"Nathaniel is not sick, I trust?" Master Clare said sharply.

"Nathaniel thrives," Charles assured his father.

"Nathaniel is your son?" Amethyst put in.

"And my grandson. I dote upon the babe so it is well that Charles and Selina have set up a separate household else he would thoroughly spoil," Master Clare said.

"My grandmother spoiled me a little, I think," Amethyst said. "She was an English lady, widowed young, and from her I received all the love I can remember from my childhood."

"But surely your lady mother – " Master Clare began.

"Oh, she has always tried to be good to me," Amethyst said hastily. "Master Schneider too! But I fear I was a sad burden to her when I was little."

"I cannot imagine Amethyst being a burden to anyone, can you, Father?" Aubrey interposed.

"She is certainly no burden as a guest," his father said. "My only worry is that she finds us rather dull. Aubrey should take her to some balls and routs and give her a taste of gaiety."

"I like best our quiet evenings," Amethyst murmured. "In company I am still somewhat shy."

"It is hardly the mark of a shy woman to leave her home and ride to visit strangers," Charles said.

"Your brother has a most persuasive tongue, sir," Amethyst said.

Her blue eyes recognised an enemy but her smile was honey sweet.

They went a few days later, to visit Charles and Selina and the baby Nathaniel. Their house was nearer the river but as oplulently furnished, though the rooms were smaller. Amethyst had prepared herself to meet an invalid, but Selina gave the lie to her husband's fretful words, being a round, rosy young woman whose conversation revolved around her child and the difficulty of finding a reliable nursemaid.

"For one simply cannot trust these wenches to look after one's child as diligently as they would look after one of their own!" she said earnestly.

"I am not yet married," Amethyst replied, smiling slightly.

"Oh, but I thought you and Aubrey – " Selina's voice

flustered into an embarrassed silence.

"Master Aubrey came into Wales to do business on his father's account," Amethyst said.

"And on whose account do you come into Chester?" Charles asked.

"My own," she answered, dimpling at him though she knew that in that quarter her smiles had no value. "I am here on my account, Master Charles."

"And do you like city life?" Selina recovered herself to enquire.

"Very much." Amethyst said brightly. "It is so quiet and dull at Foster Farm."

Quiet and dull! With the shadows long over the golden corn, and the wind piercing the high crags and Jan riding down to see her about the mill accounts, and 'Rowan Garth' set like a glowing jewel by the blue lake!

Her eyes had softened and there was yearning in the gentle curve of her mouth. Aubrey was staring at her with his own heart written clearly on his face.

Charles, glancing between the two of them, said abruptly.

"Mistress Amethyst, will you take a turn with me in the garden? I have some particularly fine vines I would like you to see."

"Shall we all go?" Selina asked.

"The sun is too hot for you, my love," Charles said.

"Aubrey, will you stay and keep Selina company for me?"

His brother, who had begun to rise, sank down again, looking faintly aggrieved.

"I will enjoy seeing your vines," Amethyst said, placing the tips of her fingers on the elder's arm.

The long garden ran down to the river and the vines were

being cultivated under glass along a broad terrace that caught the sunshine.

"Keeping a cellar of one's own wine is an excellent undertaking," Charles Clare said as they walked slowly along. "The grapes are small but sweet and the yield greater than you would expect."

"Sir, I do not think you asked me out here to talk of grapes," Amethyst said.

"No, mistress. You are right in guessing that I have something else on my mind."

"Do confide in me," she said with a touch of mischief. "Perhaps I can relieve your mind, sir."

"I hope so." He stopped short, turning to face her. "I would very much like to know your intentions regarding my brother?"

"Surely it is for someone to ask your brother his intentions regarding me," she countered.

"Aubrey is my junior by five years in age and many years more in experience," Charles said. "He was not strong in health as a child and so was kept somewhat sheltered. By nature he is shy and dreamy. We have never known him take such a keen interest in any female before. Certainly he has never brought a young lady home!"

"Is he not entitled to have friends?" she enquired.

"I would not have him hurt," Charles said.

"Hurt! You speak as if I were some hard and scheming woman," she said lightly. "I am scarce seventeen and have spent all my life in the country!"

"I will be blunt with you," he said. "I am attached to my brother and nothing would give me greater pleasure than to see him happily married to a loving wife, but I don't believe you are the right wife for him."

"Blunt indeed, Master Clare!" Her eyes flashed temper, but she kept her voice level and sweet. "I marvel that you can know so much about me after two brief meetings!"

"I pride myself on being a shrewd judge of character," he said pompously.

"I think you do both your brother and myself an injustice," she said. "Master Aubrey is neither a child nor a fool, and you must led him lead his own life. As for me, I am his good friend, as I would be yours if you would allow me. You cannot grudge me a few months' visit to Chester."

"My brother fancies himself in love with you."

"Only 'fancies'? Fancy quickly dies of its own accord."

"Not when it is encouraged!"

"Oh, am I to frown at Master Aubrey and answer him sharply?" she cried, laughing a little. "That would be a poor return for the hospitality I have been shown in your father's house!"

"If you were to marry Aubrey he would not be happy with you," Charles said.

"So now you are a prophet too! Let me set your mind at rest," she said. "At the moment I have not the slightest intention of wedding your brother. I made that clear to him before I accepted the invitation to visit Chester."

"At the moment? Then you might change your mind."

"Females have been known to do so," she murmured.

"Mistress, you are not the right wife for Aubrey," he said.

They had reached the end of the garden, where a low wall divided it from the fast-flowing river. At some distance a bridge spanned the water and, on the opposite bank, alders dipped their heads to gaze at their own reflections.

"That is not for you to say," she said.

"Mistress Amethyst, I am not as wealthy as my father," Charles said, "but I am a comfortably settled one. If I were to offer you, say, two thousand pounds to return to Wales and leave my brother to find a more suitable bride."

"You insult me," she said tightly.

"Three thousand, then? You could expand your mill handsomely with that sum!"

"I'd not take a groat! Not a farthing!" she said indignantly. "How could you, who pride yourself on your judgment of character, imagine I am the sort of woman to be bought off? I have property of my own that brings in much revenue and will provide a handsome dowry when I choose to wed. I don't need your bribe!"

"You hope to gain more from marriage with my brother? He is the younger son and will inherit the smaller share. It will be much more than three thousand, I grant you, but my father is in good health apart from his disability, and not likely to die for many years. You would be wise to accept my offer."

"I'll set your mind at rest," Amethyst said. "I have no intention of marrying Aubrey. I like him very well, but he is not the man I would choose as a husband. I decided that even before I agreed to visit Chester but you may also rest assured that, had I been inclined towards him, your words would have thrust me straight into his arms! You're a foolish man, Charles Clare!"

"Have I your word on that?" he asked gravely.

"You have my word," she said, and added haughtily. "Not that you have any right to ask for it. If I am not a suitable bride for Aubrey, then it is not your place to object but your father's."

"My father is a kindly man with a weakness for young people. He is also anxious for both his sons to be happily settled."

"Well, Master Aubrey will have to find himself another bride," she said lightly. "Indeed, I think that you may be fretting about nothing. Your brother already knows that I have no intention of wedding him. I've not told him so, for I've no wish to hurt his feelings, but I hoped, while I was in town, to meet some other young gentlemen."

"I wish you good fortune in your endeavour," he said dryly. "I have no interest in the man you eventually choose provided it is not my brother."

"Your opinion counts for very little with me," she said. "Shall we return to the house now. Your vines are pretty, sir, but I fear the grapes are somewhat sour."

She swept him a mock curtsy and set off again up the garden, her head high and her skirts rustling with the temper she was too proud to display.

"You must visit us again," Selina said cordially as they prepared to leave. "In winter we have some lively balls and suppers, even skating parties when the river is frozen. I hope you will stay longer than the summer."

"If I am pressed sufficiently I may do that," Amethyst said, smiling.

"Did you mean that?" Aubrey demanded eagerly when they had mounted up and were riding away again.

"Did I mean what?" she slanted a glance from beneath the brim of her hat.

"About staying through the winter? Would you stay until spring comes?"

"Almost a year! It would be too much of an imposition," she objected.

"It would be a pleasure, not an imposition," Aubrey said warmly. "My father and I would be delighted. Your family would permit you to stay on, wouldn't they?"

"Oh, I am left very much to my own devices by my family," she said.

"And you will stay? You will agree to spend the winter here too? Selina was right when she spoke of balls and parties."

"You go too fast, Master Aubrey!" she exclaimed. "I have made no decision one way or the other. You really must give me a little time."

"I hoped – " His fair skin crimsoned and his voice was shy. "I still feel the same way about you. I have not altered in my sentiments."

"You promised that we would not talk of such matters!"

"And I apologise for breaking my word," he said quickly. "But I am not made of stone, Amethyst. Please give me one word of hope."

"I am not able to pretend what I cannot feel," she said. "I wish I could give you more hope, but I cannot – at least, not yet. Perhaps, if I were to stay on a few months more, it might be possible for me to give you a more definite answer."

"And I must rest content with that?" His face and voice were full of disappointment.

"If you are not prepared to do so, then it would be better for me to go home at the end of summer," she said unyieldingly.

"Please stay," he urged. "I'll not importune you further, I swear. Write to your lady mother and ask her if you may stay until the spring."

"Well, we'll see," she said in a kindlier tone, smiling at him before she urged Cariad ahead.

She was not sure if she wanted to extend her visit or not. The Clares, save for Charles, had welcomed her but there was no doubt that it would be hard to justify a visit that lasted for a year unless at the end of it she agreed either to a marriage or a betrothal. It might be worth it simply to spite Charles, she thought with an inward grin. The elder of the Clare sons had distrusted her on sight for no reason she could fathom. Perhaps there was some arrangement whereby Aubrey's allowance was increased when he married, and so Charles would object to any woman who took his brother's fancy. She could not picture any man disliking her on sight.

"It might be pleasant to go to skating parties," she said thoughtfully. "At home the cold weather blocks the passes and brings no joy of any kind, but here in town I suppose life is easier even in winter."

"I would have life easy for you all the time," Aubrey said.

His face and voice were full of wistful hope, but she ignored the unspoken plea, crying merrily,

"How dull that would be! Struggle spices existence!"

One day her own struggle would be done and Jan would take her as she had always planned. One day there would be no Isobel to stand between. To stay away for a whole year would be the hardest thing she had ever done, but it might be the wisest. There would be the bleakness of the winter and all the fuss and bother attending the birth of the new babe for Jan to endure, without even the occasional conversation with her or visit to Foster Farm to alleviate his misery. When she returned in the spring he would no longer be able to resist the temptation she so sweetly offered.

"I will wait a week or two," she said carelessly over her shoulder, "and then write to my lady mother and ask her leave to extend the length of my visit – if your father will not object?"

"He will be as pleased as I am," Aubrey assured her and his delight beamed in his face.

# Ten

Isobel had agreed to allow Amethyst to extend her visit so readily that the girl sensed a fervent relief in every line of the letter.

"My dear Amethyst," she had written, "Your recent communication arrived safely and we were delighted to learn that you continue to enjoy yourself. It is most kind of the Clares to extend their hospitality for a further term and you must certainly accept. It is my opinion that every young lady should have a season in town, and I hope you will take advantage of the opportunities afforded.

"Our own news is scant. Mair Bohanna is with child, expected some time in the spring. I am in good health but very fat! Myfi has not been well at all. Age is catching her up, I fear. Lowell is growing apace. By the time you return in the spring he will be walking, I've no doubt.

Your affectionate mother

Isobel Schneider."

No word of Jan or from him. Amethyst folded the letter away with a grimace.

At least she could fill her days with activities and at night she was usually too tired to lie awake for long. Only her dreams were troubling and most of them blurred on waking. She spent much of her time in riding Cariad across the fields beyond the town walls, usually with Aubrey in devoted attendance, and she accompanied him to local gaieties when the younger members of the gentry went picnicking down by the river or hired boats to punt idly over the rushing water. The evenings were spent mainly in the house apart from an occasional visit to some neighbouring family, and Amethyst preferred the quiet times. The study where Master Clare spent his days held a fascination for her. She liked to sit watching the firelight dance over the surfaces of the polished tables and chairs, the gleaming spines of the leather-bound books, the badly painted portrait with the jar of flowers placed beneath it as if in tribute. It was interesting to hear father and son discussing the business while she sat quietly in the corner, her chin on her hand, her eyes moving between the two.

The summer was dying. In the town one didn't notice the summer dying but her mind leapt back to Pen Tân so often that she knew, without seeing, exactly when the leaves began to change colour and the sheep to grow their winter fleeces. Within the dim, richly furnished house the seasons slid unnoticed one into the other. Only when one rode out in the fields or through the narrow streets did one become conscious of a nip in the wind, a paling of the blue sky. Harvest had come and gone and there was a sharp October on the horizon.

"The months fly by so quickly," Richard Clare observed.

"Not for me," she answered, caught off her guard by his casual remark.

"Are you beginning to find the town dull?" he asked.

"No, indeed!" she said. "I find time passes slowly everywhere."

"That's because you're young," he said wryly. "At my age days flash past like hours. Where is Aubrey?"

"He had some work to make up," Amethyst said. "I believe he went over to see Master Charles."

"You ought to have gone with him, not stayed here by yourself."

"I am not by myself," she said cordially, "I am with you."

"That's very kind of you, my dear. I fear I am poor company for a pretty young girl."

"Master Charles doesn't approve of me," Amethyst said. "He has made it clear."

"He is fond of Aubrey, and he does not take easily to strangers," the other said. "You must not take it too personally, child."

"I don't wish to intrude where I am not wanted," she said.

"You are most welcome to stay with us," he said, but there was a faint reservation in his tone.

"But?" She stared at him, her delicate brows raised.

"I, too, am fond of Aubrey," he said. "He is, after all, my younger son. I am anxious for his happiness too."

"Are you going to ask me my intentions?" she enquired lightly.

"Aubrey is – greatly attracted to you," Master Clare said, lacing his fingers together. "He has not said anything to me but I know my son. He never invited a young lady to visit us before, and your wanting to stay through the winter – "

"You said I was welcome!"

"Most welcome, my dear, but when spring comes, what then?" His glance was suddenly penetrating.

"I am not going to marry Aubrey," she said flatly. "I am not going to marry anyone, ever!"

"My dear girl, why not?" He looked at her in astonishment. "You are not yet eighteen! What has decided you against marriage?"

"I can never marry," she said, her head drooping.

"Why not?" he persisted.

"I have bad blood in me," she said dolefully.

"Child, what are you talking about? Jan Schneider is one of the finest men I know!"

"Jan Schneider is not my father," she said, raising her head, speaking with conscious gallantry. "My mother was raped by her own brother and I was born. My father was my uncle too, he was mad, raving mad, and hanged himself before I was born. The tale was hushed up in the district and when my mother married Jan Schneider it was pretended that he was my real father. Many people believe the tale, and in another generation there will be nobody left who knows the truth."

"But you know it."

"It was necessary for me to know," she said sadly. "I can never risk bearing children, you see, and that means I can never marry. I am doomed to remain an old maid all my life, living on Foster Farm with a housekeeper companion, growing older and lonelier. My mother doesn't like me have to visit her too often. I remind her of what she wishes to forget. So I took advantage of Master Aubrey's invitation to visit Chester, so that I might store up a little gaiety before I return."

"My dear Amethyst!" His fine-drawn aristocratic features were tight with distress. "You bear a heavy legacy!"

"Oh, I have no legacy at all," she said. "Foster Farm was left me by my grandmother but all the rest will go to my half-brother, Lowell. Lord knows I don't grudge the darling babe anything! He is the sweetest little boy! But I have only the mill and though the profits are good I know that business is always a risk. Jan looks after my affairs and is very good to me but he cannot live for ever and there's the farm to occupy most of his time. I shall have to begin to take an interest in the mill very soon, and I am a fool about such things!"

"I am sure Master Schneider has taken that into consideration," Master Clare said.

"Oh, he has been very good to me," she said earnestly. "I am most grateful to him for his kindness. But you do understand that it's impossible for me to wed? I would take it as a kindness from you if you did not mention this to your sons. My mother would die of shame if she thought that her sad history had become public property."

"I will say nothing," he said briefly, but he put out his hand, pressing her shoulder in a gesture of sympathy that caused genuine tears to flood her eyes.

"I have made it clear to Master Aubrey that I am not prepared to consider marriage with him," she said. "It has been selfish of me to expect to remain here. I can see that now. Naturally, I will make arrangements to leave within the next few days. It would be wrong to keep his hopes alive by remaining here, and I could not possibly tell him the truth."

"You go too fast," he said, his voice overriding her own gently regretful tone. "You have been frank with me and that I appreciate very much, but you must give me a little time to think."

"To think about what, sir?" She twisted around to face him. "I can never marry Aubrey. I can never marry any man. To stay here would be to take advantage of your hospitality and offer no return. After all, I have had the summer here to remember."

"You could stay and marry me," he said.

"I beg your pardon?" she said faintly.

"You could marry me," he repeated. "You tell me that you cannot risk having children. Well, I am incapable of fathering them, incapable since my accident of pleasuring any woman. As my wife that part of marriage would be closed to you, but you would enjoy the privileges and position of a wife. You would be mistress of a fine house with an assured future, and no risk of being labelled a spinster."

"To become your wife?"

"Is the idea repugnant to you?" he asked, a touch of sadness in his voice.

"No, of course not!" She reached to touch the back of his hand, her eyes brilliant with unshed tears. "I am most flattered by your offer, sir, but I fear you make it out of pity."

"Not so, unless it be pity for myself," he said. "I have been a very lonely man since my dear wife died. She was a gentle soul – Aubrey takes after her. Charles is more like me. He has the shrewder business sense. But I am a man who enjoys female company. Perhaps you would find it very dull to be tied to a man not only much older than yourself but bound to a wheelchair?"

"I find the company of younger men sadly tiresome at times," she said. "Perhaps it is nature's way of preparing me for the life I must lead."

"It would not be a life without affection," he said. "I have grown accustomed to your company. I must confess it has been my wish to see you married to Aubrey partly because it would mean your staying here. You see I am not entirely unselfish."

"Even if it were possible," she said. "I would not be the right wife for Master Aubrey. He needs a more managing sort of woman, one who would spur him on and increase his self-confidence. I was never a very managing sort of girl."

"You are a very sweet girl. I am not surprised my son is taken with you."

"He will find another girl to love," Amethyst said.

"And I cannot guarantee that I will even like her. In any case, they would set up their own establishment and then I would be truly alone."

"Oh, sir, we would both be alone!" she cried softly. "You here in this house and I at Foster Farm."

"With the estimable Mistress Jenkins."

"Exactly!" She brushed her hand across her eyes and laughed shakily.

"I advised you to take some time before you decided whether to go or stay," he said. "Now I offer you another alternative and find myself as impatient as a boy to hear your answer."

"Master Clare, I would give you my answer at once," she said, "but one consideration holds me back."

"You think your lady mother would object to the match?"

"She would not object to my marrying a man like yourself."

"A cripple you mean?" He spoke without bitterness.

"You will not tell her that you know the truth?"

"I will say nothing," he promised, "but you may make it clear that our marriage will be in name only, to set her fears at rest."

"That isn't why I hesitate," she said, lowering her eyes modestly. "It is simply that – sir, you have two sons already and they will expect to inherit when you die. How will they take it if you wed again?"

"My life is my own affair," he said querulously. "I do not need to ask their permission to do what I wish to do with my own life!"

"I would not wish to cheat them of anything," she murmured.

"You are a good wench," he said, his eyes warm as they rested on her. "I have made a good choice of a bride. But my sons must not depend entirely on me for their security. They must run their own affairs when I am gone, increase the profits of the business through their own endeavours. However, I will set your mind at rest. While I am alive, if you agree to marry me, you will receive my protection as is due to my wife. When I die you will receive the sum of ten thousand pounds. That is fair and not excessive. My sons would really have no right to object to that."

"It sounds most generous," she said.

"Generous but not extravagant. You could use such an inheritance to expand and improve your mill if you decided to return to Wales after my death."

"I beg you not to talk so lightly of your death," she pleaded. "I would sorely miss your company!"

"You are a kind little thing," he said, smiling at her. "But you might easily be widowed when you are still a young woman, and I want you to be assured that you would be left independent.''

"There is the question of my dowry," she began.

"Keep it as my wedding gift," he said. "What of your mill? Will Master Schneider continue to manage it?"

"If I wed you – I have not yet given my answer."

"How much time will you need?" he asked.

"This is not a matter of business to be concluded without emotion," she protested. "You must put yourself in my place, sir. I am offered a way out of my difficulties which tempts me greatly, but I fear you have made it on the spur of the moment and may regret it. And I must confess that my thoughts are not entirely on the subject of my own marriage. My lady mother expects another babe at any time and if, God forbid, anything were to happen to her, I might then be required at home to keep house for my stepfather."

"Your scruples do you great credit," he approved. "We will delay your answer then until word comes from Wales? I shall pray for your mother's safe delivery."

"Oh, I shall be praying too," she assured him. She doubted if she had ever prayed more fervently. If Isobel died then Jan would have no choice but to summon her home and it would cause great scandal if she did not keep house for him. She dared not risk marriage until she was certain there was no other way to gain what she wanted. What she wanted more than anything was Jan and Pen Tân – the two were bound together, but if she could obtain neither then she would comfort herself with money.

The prospect of wedding Richard Clare held a certain charm. There would be no need to endure any embrace more intimate than a kiss, and it would be an excellent way of paying out Charles for his baseless suspicions of her. Of

Aubrey she decided not to think.

More than a week passed before a letter arrived. Amethyst read it in her room, sat for a long time willing her bright anger to subside, and then went with carefully composed face down to the study. Richard Clare was seated at the desk, immersed as usual in his ledgers but he looked up with a smile as she tapped on the half-open door.

"Come in, my dear. No need to stand upon ceremony. You received a letter?"

"From my stepfather," she nodded, apricot skirts rustling as she seated herself. "He writes that my lady mother has been delivered of a boy, a little before its time as was Lowell, but both are doing well. The new babe is to be named Prester."

"Stay on in Chester as long as you choose," Jan had written. "I am pleased that you are happy there and we look forward to news of a betrothal very shortly. Your mother joins with me in sending love."

So he was pleased that she was still away and looked forward to news of a betrothal! Well, she was ready to satisfy his desire.

"My lady mother is a fortunate woman," she said sweetly. "Two little babes and a loving husband."

"Would you have wanted children, had circumstances been different?" Richard Clare asked abruptly.

"I never thought much about it." She put her finger to her lips, considering, and then shook her head. "I don't believe I am the maternal sort of girl. Does that sound a dreadful thing to say?"

"An honest thing. Your honesty is one of the most refreshing qualities about you," he said.

"And my mother is well, so I am not needed at home."

"Does that mean you are prepared to consider my offer?" his voice was suddenly very eager.

"You do not regret making it? It has not been mentioned between us since."

"I wanted to give you time to consider," he said. "I wanted you to be sure, perfectly sure."

"I am sure." She raised her head, her blue eyes steady on his face. "I am sure, Master Clare. I would be most happy to be your wife."

"My dear Amethyst, how pleased I am to hear you say that!" he exclaimed. "I must confess that I have waited with great inward impatience for your answer."

"I would like to be married very quietly and soon," Amethyst murmured. "Your son – Master Charles, I mean – will try to prevent it."

"Neither of my sons have any influence over my life," he said sharply. "You may safely leave them to me."

"I will write to my mother and tell her that we are to be quietly wed. I am certain she will not refuse her consent."

"Would you like Master Schneider to come and give you away?"

"No!" She spoke quickly, her colour rising. "No, I won't drag him away from the new babe at the start of the winter season. We'll be quietly and privately wed."

"Then we must find you a betrothal ring at least."

"A ring?" She glanced down at the serpent ring, wondering why she should feel such distaste of wearing another. The serpent gave her a sense of identity, for when she looked at it she was reminded of ancestors long gone who no longer needed to suffer, no longer had any power over the living.

"A ring is customary," Richard Clare said gently.

"But this is not the customary sort of marriage," she said. "Naturally, I shall expect to wear your wedding ring, but a betrothal ring – it seems strange somehow."

"Go to the cabinet by the window," he instructed. "The second drawer down. There is a flat case there – bring it to me."

Obediently she did as she was told, laying the flat box on the desk before him. He lifted the lid and beckoned her close, his expression pleased when he saw her own.

"It's beautiful!" Her eyes were sparkling as she, at his nod, drew out the necklace of amethyst set in gold.

"I ordered it some weeks ago," he said, "hoping to give it to you either as a parting gift or when you married Aubrey. Now you can wear it in lieu of a betrothal ring, if you will honour me so far."

"It is most kind of you!" On impulse she bent and kissed him, the necklace still wound about her hand.

"You deserve a great deal more," he said, patting her shoulder. "You displayed great courage in telling me your sad history. Many a young woman would have married Aubrey and said nothing."

"I could not risk having a babe," she said, "It would be most unfair on any man I wed. The poor thing might be a monster."

"The possibility will not even arise," he said reassuringly. "You will make that clear when you write to your lady mother? I will not mention anything of it myself, of course."

"You are very good to me." She experienced a glow of

real gratitude as she fastened the amethyst about her throat.
"I shall be a good wife to you, Master Clare."

"You must call me Richard now," he said.

"Richard, then." She retreated a pace, sunlight glinting
on the blue stones through a gap in the heavy curtains. "Will
you tell your sons of our plans to wed? I must confess to
some nervousness as to how they will take the information."

"I will make all right," he said.

As she returned to her chamber she thought that he
probably would. Despite his disability there was a
commanding air about him, a hidden strength of purpose.
He had in many ways a ruthlessness to match her own, for
he had disregarded his son's feelings in proposing to her.
Such selfishness was to be admired – and watched.

She sat down to write her letter, tongue flicking her lips as
she composed the careful sentences.

"My dear mother,

It was with the utmost joy that I heard of your recent safe
delivery of yet another little brother. I rejoice for you both. I
have news of my own to impart which may not come as a
complete surprise, especially since I decided to extend my
visit. Master Richard Clare has done me the honour of
asking for my hand in marriage and I, being certain of your
consent, have accepted him. As he is in uncertain health the
wedding will be a very quiet and private affair, but I will
embark on my new life secure in the knowledge of your
blessing. I have no doubt that Richard will be writing to you
himself, but I may tell you now that he has refused to accept
any dowry, I am most grateful to him for his generosity. I
hope that Jan will continue to manage the mill at Foster
Farm. It will be some time, you will appreciate, before I am

able to visit you. Chester holds so much that is interesting and new that it will be a long time before I exhaust its delights."

She broke off, frowning as the door was thrust open and Aubrey appeared on the threshold.

"Is it true?" His voice and hands shook and the colour came and went in his face. "My father has just now told me – is it true?"

"That he and I are to wed? Perfectly true."

"It cannot be! When I made an offer for your hand – "

"I refused it."

"On the contrary, you gave me no answer at all!" he interrupted. "You offered me your friendship and bade me have patience. I was led to believe you might alter your mind."

"I have altered it," she said. "I have decided to marry Richard."

"He's an old man! You cannot seriously intend to marry an old man!"

"I prefer older men," she said serenely.

"Amethyst, you cannot mean what you say." He was staring at her in consternation. "You are a beautiful girl any man would be proud to claim as a wife. You cannot mean to tie yourself to a cripple."

"He is your father – "

"And I love him dearly, but that cannot alter the facts. He is confined to a wheelchair and cannot pleasure a woman."

"You cannot be certain of that," she flashed. "I would swear that 'tis not a subject you have ever discussed with him. You simply took it for granted that he was incapable of marrying again."

"But why would you agree to wed him?" Aubrey asked. "You have every right to refuse me, but why choose a man so much older? He could be your grandsire!"

"Instead of which he is to be my husband."

"I cannot believe it." His thin face was ashen now. "Am I so repugnant to you? I hoped you had come to care for me."

"I am very fond of you," she said, "but I have grown more deeply attached to your father. I have said nothing because I was not certain of the strength of his own feelings for me. I hoped he had begun to care – "

"Without the slightest regard for me!"

"How childish you sound!" she said scornfully. "Anyone would imagine you were the only one to be considered! I am deeply fond of your father. You have no right to criticise either of us or to speak out against our marriage. We are free to do as we please. My mother has given me permission to wed where I choose and my choice is Richard, as I am his."

"And I am expected to accept you as my stepmother!"

"You may do as you please," Amethyst said loftily.

"I'll not continue to live here," he said.

"Our marriage doesn't depend on that," she said. "Perhaps it would be as well if you went and resided with your brother until you found a wife of your own."

"I thought I had found one," he said, and looked abruptly so young and hurt that she felt a pang of pity.

"I never gave you cause," she said more gently. "In time I hope we can be friends again. I want us to be friends. But if you cannot accept the marriage then there's an end to it."

"Will nothing change your mind?" he pleaded.

"Nothing." Her voice was firm and her hand steady as she gripped the pen more tightly. "And I would be obliged if you would refrain from bursting in upon me unannounced. I am sure you were not reared so."

She kept her eyes lowered and, when the door had slammed behind him, she returned to the writing of her letter.

## Eleven

In three months time, Amethyst reflected, she would be nineteen years old, and for the past sixteen months she had been Mistress Clare. She glanced across the study at the portrait hanging on the wall and wondered if the first Mistress Clare had been as bored as she was after so brief a time. Probably not, for Richard's first wife had been a gentle soul who liked sewing and was happy to sit day after day waiting for her lord and master to throw her a word.

In that she was aware she was being unfair to Richard, who never acted towards her otherwise than with the utmost kindness and courtesy. He was a good man, she knew, but he was a man who had been set in his ways for many years and had no intention of allowing anyone to alter them. It had not even been necessary for her to take over the reins of the household. The manservants saw to everything with a quiet and quelling competence, and on the few occasions that she ventured into the kitchen she was treated as if she were a guest.

There was no private life between her and her husband. Richard occupied his solitary chamber and had his personal needs attended to by his valet. The only task she was permitted to perform was to wheel his chair from study to bedroom or down the sloping passage to the dining-room. On fine afternoons he was occasionally persuaded into the garden for an hour, and, more rarely, he was lifted into his carriage and driven down to his shop or to one of the warehouses where his bales were stored. Charles and Aubrey seldom came near and, when they did, Amethyst made it her business to keep to her own quarters. She would not soon forget the unpleasantness that had surrounded her marriage. Aubrey had moved out to live in his brother's house and, on the rare occasions they had met since, he had been silent and sulky. Charles had never exchanged a sentence with her, but she had heard him and his father arguing, their voices sharp, bitter and curiously alike.

She could have endured the hostility of the sons, but the marriage had caused something of a scandal among the close-knit circle of Master Clare's acquaintances. That he should marry a young girl who had come to the house at his son's invitation had struck the gentlemen as ribald, the ladies as faintly shocking. There had been no invitations issued to the newly wedded couple, and Richard Clare had reacted with cool disdain.

"We do not require their permission or their approval, my dear. It is fortunate that you are not a young lady who craves constant gaieties. We have each other."

He made it sound idyllic, but the reality was less so. The evenings were interminable when he sat reading or writing, glancing up occasionally to smile at her in an absent-minded fashion where she sat, the same page of her book open on her lap while her eyes read the same sentence over and over. It never occurred to him, she thought resentfully, that her tapping foot craved music for a dance and that her hand, curved over her mouth, concealed the most excruciating boredom.

What had hurt her almost beyond bearing was the readiness with which permission for her to wed had been given. Isobel had made no secret of her relief in getting a difficult daughter off her hands, even Jan had written in glowing terms, wishing her every happiness. Deep down she had hoped that he might forbid the match, even ride post-haste to Chester to beg her to return to Wales. Instead, there had been a letter in which she could discern no trace of regret or yearning. It was as if he had slammed a door shut in her face.

The wedding had had a bleakness that was not entirely due to the time of year. The minister had come to the house to perform the ceremony and only Walton, Richard's valet, and Mistress Jenkins had witnessed their taking of the vows, and afterwards they had drunk wine and eaten iced cake and Amethyst had tried to feel like a married woman. At least she had not been forced to share a bed with her bridegroom. She had retained her own chamber and found the long nights there a welcome respite from the evening's boredom. In the privacy of her room, the bolt on the door drawn against any possible intrusion from Mistress Jenkins, she could lie with closed eyes on the bed and pretend that Jan cradled her in his arms, whispering that he could no longer live without her. Every imagined scene was as vivid as reality in her mind, but as month followed month reality became harder to bear.

At least she had a generous allowance with nothing to spend it on except clothes.

"I am," she informed her mirror, "the most expensively dressed lady who was never invited out in the world!"

Her reflection smiled brightly back at her, lips red over gleaming white teeth, curls cunningly tousled under a confection of ribbons and straw, a gown of claret silk faced with palest pink outlining her figure. She had grown more lovely since her marriage, but sometimes she feared that her beauty would fade just as swiftly in this dim and silent house. Only when she made the effort to go out in the garden or saddle Cariad for a gallop did she realise fully that it was high spring and that her blood sang with the season though nobody heard. She supposed that any other woman in her position would have found a lover, but the only lover she ever wanted was forbidden to her.

There was a tap on the door and Mistress Jenkins came in, a letter in her hand and on her face the mixture of trepidation and excitement with which she greeted any missive.

"From Pen Tân, Mistress Amethyst! It will be word of the new babe."

"So it will. I had forgotten it was due," Amethyst lied.

That her mother, at forty, should be expecting yet another child had struck Amethyst as disgusting. Isobel, she thought as she broke the seal on the letter, was nothing more than a brood mare.

The note was in Jan's hand.

"My dear Amethyst,

It is with the greatest regret that I take up my pen to inform you that Isobel, your loving mother and my entirely beloved wife, died in childbed in the early hours of yesterday. The babe, a girl, has survived but as yet, I can take small comfort in the fact. I am desolated by my loss but will write more fully when I am more collected.

Jan."

"From the look on your face it's good news," Mistress Jenkins said.

"I have a little sister," Amethyst told her.

"A daughter for Mistress Isobel! Oh, how pleased they will be!"

"My mother died," Amethyst said shortly.

"Died? Oh, no!" Mistress Jenkins's eyes filled with tears.

"It's very sad," Amethyst nodded, "but we must think of my poor little half-brothers and sister. They are left without a mother to care for them."

"And poor Master Schneider to be widowed! Oh, it will break his heart, for he was devoted to your mother."

"As you say." Amethyst spoke somewhat shortly, not wishing to hear the extent of Jan's affection for Isobel.

"And ideal couple! I said as much when they wed," the housekeeper mourned. "They had such a short space of time together!"

"Yes, didn't they?" Amethyst's red lips curled slightly as she folded the letter.

"You will require a mourning dress. Shall I lay one out?"

"Later. I must answer this." She moved swiftly to the table and took up pen and paper. "Is the postboy still here?"

"Having some cake and ale in the kitchen."

"Take this down to him so that he can start back swiftly."

She scribbled the brief reply, her hand shaking in her eagerness.

"Dear Jan,

I am returning to Wales as soon as possible,

Yours,

Amethyst."

Sanding and sealing it she said, impatience in her voice.

"I will require a new mourning dress and so will you. Go into the town and order material from the shop. Black lace and ribbons too. Mistress Collins can make them up speedily."

"Is there anything else?" Mistress Jenkins asked, sniffing dolefully.

"I will tell Master Clare what has happened. He will be most distressed, for he knew Master Schneider and so will share in his grief."

"As we all do," Mistress Jenkins said. "At a time like this we learn the value of sympathy. When my Sam, God rest his soul!, died I was so grateful for the expressions of friendship that came my way, so grateful."

"Hurry with the letter," Amethyst said. "I must go to Master Clare. This has been a shock for me too. After her safe confinements my mother might have been expected to get through this one without harm."

"The Good Lord does not always heed our prayers," Mistress Jenkins said.

"Oh, sometimes he does," Amethyst murmured piously. Mistress Jenkins bestowed on her another commiserating glance and went out.

Isobel dead! Amethyst sat down on the edge of the bed and stared into space, wonderment in her eyes. Four years of the most fervent prayers and she had finally been answered. She bent her head, clasping her hands together, and sent up thanks. To her surprise her lashes were damp. Perhaps, after all, she had been fond of her mother. The thought pleased her because it seemed to prove that she was really a much nicer person than she suspected.

After a few moments she rose and ran lightly down the stairs to the study. Richard sat there in his usual place, head inclined to the door as she entered. He wore his own greying hair and the thin shaft of sunlight falling on his face revealed the lines engraved on the sallow, fine-drawn features.

"Come in, my dear." He spoke with his customary politeness. "I thought you were going out for a ride."

"I've had word from home," she said, ignoring his faintly raised brows at her use of the word 'home'. "My lady mother has died giving birth to a girl child."

"My dear, I am so very sorry!" He held out his hand to her, concern on his face.

"A letter came informing me of the sad event," she said.

"Master Schneider will be disconsolate. I know only too well how crushing a blow the loss of a beloved wife can be."

His gaze moved to the portrait on the wall.

"He is left with three small children to rear," she said.

"Lowell is not yet three and Prester only sixteen months and the new babe – oh, it is too sad to contemplate!"

"I am most deeply sorry," he repeated, patting her hand.

She withdrew her fingers gently from his grasp and sat down on the window seat.

"I have sent word that I will be returning home as soon as possible," she said.

This time he caught her up on the words, echoing it. "Home? My dear, your home is here now."

"To Pen Tân then," she said impatiently.

"The funeral will be over by now," he pointed out. "There is nothing you could do."

"Jan is alone, alone and grieving!" she protested.

"Then invite him to visit us here," Richard said, "a change of scene may be just what he needs to take his mind off the recent tragedy."

"He would not leave the children," Amethyst said. "They are so little, and now left motherless. I must go home at once."

"Your sentiments do you credit, my dear, but they are not rooted in common sense," he pointed out. "The children are too small to grieve and by now some good, reliable nurse will have been found for them. Your lady mother, God rest her soul!, is in her grave. Your return will do nothing."

"Jan is alone," she said.

"And for that I am sorry, truly sorry, which is why I suggested your inviting him here for a while."

"He would not come. Apart from the children there is the spring sowing. There is the mill to be managed. You know I have not seen my own property since I came to Chester."

"From all you have said I was not aware that you took much interest in your property," he said wryly. "I am sorry for your loss, but I cannot drop everything at a moment's notice and travel to Wales. Even if my business affairs didn't make it impossible I doubt if I am capable of making such a journey. It's many years since I left Chester. You know that Aubrey always travelled on my business."

"Oh, I would not expect you to come with me!" she exclaimed. "You cannot possibly make such a journey!"

"You surely didn't mean to go by yourself?" he

questioned sharply, leaning forward to peer at her more intently.

"Women do travel abroad. We are not living in the Dark Ages! And I would naturally hire escort."

"My wife would not have dreamed of going anywhere without me."

"You were not in a wheelchair then," she said coldly.

"Had I been she would have been difficult to persuade away from my side."

"She's dead and I am your wife now," she countered.

"And I did not marry you to have you run off into Wales whenever the fancy takes you. I married you for company, my dear. Surely you will not deprive me of it now?"

"Your sons – " she began.

"Charles and Aubrey speak with me only when business makes it necessary," he said. "My wedding to you ended all friendship between them and myself."

"That was not my fault! I warned you how it would be."

"And I was content to have it so. But I gave up a great deal for your sake. You cannot turn your back on me now."

"Why, you talk as if I were running off for ever!" she laughed. "A month or two. I ask only a month or two, merely to condole with my – my stepfather and see the babes. I would be back by Harvest."

"I seem to recall you coming here in springtime," he said, "and you planned then to return to Wales for the Harvest Feast. You have not been back since."

"All the more reason for me to return now!" she flashed.

"All the less reason to leave your home and husband. It is never wise to look over your shoulder, my dear, at what is past and gone."

"So you will not allow me to go?" Amethyst spoke calmly, her fists clenched in the folds of her gown.

"It is not a question of my forbidding you," he said. "You are upset about your mother and your first inclination is to rush home! It is only natural but you will see when you have thought a little that you do no good by wanting to go back to Wales. Your arrival would only remind him of what he has lost. In a year or so I see no reason why you should not go back for a visit. By then I may be on better terms with Charles and Aubrey."

He believed that he was speaking the truth, she thought, trying to be fair, but he deceived himself as much as he tried to deceive her. He had given her the name of wife and in return for that she was held virtual prisoner in this dim, luxurious house, chained to a man who was himself bound in a chair. An old man, she thought bitterly, incapable of pleasuring her even if she had wanted it. If only she had waited a little longer than a year she need not have married anyone. She ought to have had more faith in the prayers she had poured out.

"I'm sorry, my dear, if you are disappointed," he was saying. "I will write to Master Schneider myself and suggest that he pays us a visit as soon as he is able to do so. You will need a mourning gown, I know."

"Mistress Jenkins has gone down to see about that."

"An admirable woman! She will have been shocked at your sad news too."

"Very shocked." She answered him levelly, her hands still clenched.

"You must not be too impatient with me." For the first time there was a note of pleading in his voice. "I am very dependent on your company, my love. Very grateful to have such a charming young wife."

"You're very kind," she said, making her customary response.

It would always be thus. He would turn her into a pale copy of his first wife and she would spend the rest of her life thanking him for his kindness. Amethyst turned her head aside, pulling the curtain, so that she could look down into the garden. It was gay with spring flowers but she had only to avert her eyes a fraction to see the long, cobbled street and high walls of the neighbouring houses. Everywhere she turned there were walls closing in upon her and when she looked back into the room she could see only the man in the wheelchair and the portrait hanging on the wall. The sudden, terrifying conviction came to her that if she looked closely at the portrait she would see her own face looking back at her.

"I have been foolish," she said slowly. "Naturally, you don't want me to leave you and travel all the way to Wales! I would do no good by going there – and I fear I would miss you as much as you would miss me."

"You're a sensible girl." He gave her the smile that she had begun to find patronising.

"Would you like to go out in the garden for a little while?" she asked. "I am – restless. The bad news has shaken me badly. My poor mother was only forty years old, and she had borne her other babes safely. I cannot even weep for her yet."

"It is the shock. Grief affects people in different ways."

"Will you come into the garden? I would like your company for a while," she repeated patiently.

"Of course, my dear. If you call Collins he can help me down."

"No need. I can manage the chair down the ramp and we can go through the dining-room. I like," she added wistfully, "to feel useful."

"Very well, my dear." He patted her hand again as she came to his side.

The corridor ran past the head of the stairs towards the steep passage that led into the dining-room. She had pushed the wheelchair down the ramp once or twice but usually the valet was at hand to take Richard Clare where he wished to go.

"Take it slowly," he cautioned. "I will hold the handrail along the wall to help you."

"Yes." She spoke gently, sweat breaking out on the palms of her hands as she gripped the handle of the chair.

It ran easily, silently, along the thick carpet. The corridor was gloomy, a small lamp casting faint illumination upon them. She had reached the head of the staircase now. These, too, were carpeted and a sudden misgiving assailed her. If they had been stone there would have been no uncertainty.

"Why have you stopped?" Richard asked, turning his head to look up at her.

Risks sometimes had to be taken. She swivelled the chair so that it faced the top step, heaved an enormous sigh that sent her breath whistling out of her body and pushed. Richard cried out something; the wheels of the chair teetered on the step; man and chair crashed down, banging against wall and banisters as they went.

She stood for an instant, marvelling at the ease of it all, and then began to scream. It was easy to scream. The sounds bubbled up in her throat, emerged on a continuous, high-pitched note, filling the narrow passage with sound that echoed and re-echoed, beating against her ears.

People were running from various parts of the house. She was aware of shocked voices, cries of dismay. Her own screams were growing fainter and thinner and her head was hurting, pain stabbing at her temples and behind her eyes.

"Mistress Clare!"

Someone was shaking her. She dimly recognised Collins, the valet, and leaned against him.

"The physician must be called," she heard herself say.

"Mistress, it would do no good. The master is dead. The fall broke his neck," Collins was saying.

"No! No, it can't be so!"

"What happened, mistress? How did the master come to fall?" the valet asked.

"It was my fault," she said shiveringly. "My fault! We were going to the dining-room and Richard thought he heard a noise in the hall below. We paused to look down and I let go of the chair. I let go of the chair for one second and it tipped. It tipped over the edge and Richard fell. It was my fault!"

She began to cry helplessly, tears pouring down her face. She was not sure if she was crying for her mother, or for the necessity she had had of pushing Richard Clare down the stairs, or for Jan who was all alone at Pen Tân with three motherless babes. Perhaps, more than anything, she was crying for herself. Life had been unfair, depriving her of the man she loved, forcing her into actions that, in the deepest part of herself, she could never seek to justify.

Someone was leading her to her bedchamber. She

recognised Collins and, seeing the grief on the valet's sombre features, sobbed more violently, repeating over and over, "My fault! My fault!"

"Mistress, you cannot blame yourself," Collins said urgently. "It was a sad accident."

"Richard is dead! My husband is dead!" she wrung her hands.

"I'll send Mistress Jenkins to you," the valet said.

"She went into the town," Amethyst sobbed.

At least there would be no need to order fresh mourning. What she wore for Isobel would do equally well for Richard.

# Epilogue

"But you cannot possibly stay here," Jan said.

"Not stay!" Amethyst echoed him in hurt astonishment. "Where else will I go, pray? Back to Chester? My loving stepsons as good as accused me of pushing poor Richard down the stairs on purpose!"

"There is Foster Farm. That is your property still. I've made it ready for your occupation."

"So!" She drew a long, quivering breath. "I am to live down at Foster Farm and you are to live here at 'Rowan Garth'. Where is the sense in that? Who will take care of you now? Myfi is dead and Jane too feeble to work more than a few hours a day. You have three children and you need a woman."

"Not in the way you mean it," he said sharply.

"Why, what way could I mean it?" she asked, innocently widening her eyes at him. Above the high collar of her black dress her face was pale and perfect, crowned with its aureole of red curls.

"Amethyst, I'm not a fool!" he exclaimed. "You're a very lovely and wealthy young widow and half the gallants in the neighbourhood will be beating a path to your door."

"I don't want any of them!"

"I know that too. I've not forgotten the scene between us – "

"Must you remind me of past humiliation?" she interrupted. "I am older now."

"And even more desirable."

"Do you truly think so?" she asked eagerly.

"You must know that I do," he said.

"Yet we sit here with the width of the parlour separating us."

"As it must always be so," he said.

"But I would not ask for me," she said eagerly. "I was brought up in this house, Jan. I left only because you wed my mother and I couldn't bear to witness your happiness. I have a right to be here to take care of you. My mother would have wished it."

"It's the last thing Isobel would have wished."

"All I ask is to be allowed to take care of the household," she begged. "I could look after Lowell and Prester and little Rowan. They need a woman. Isn't it better for them to have their half-sister rear them than a stranger? And we could sit together in the evenings, talk, play cards."

"You think it would end at talking?" There was a sudden harshness in his voice. "You're fooling yourself, my dear. Before a month was out you would be trying to seduce me."

"If I did you could always refuse," she said, mischief in her eyes.

"Make no mistake about it." The harshness remained in his voice and his own glance was level. "I would always refuse. I bear your mother's memory too much honour to betray it. I would always refuse and your affection for me would turn into bitterness and finally to hatred. That would be no atmosphere in which to rear young children or to live ourselves."

"You set yourself up as a prophet," she said sourly.

"Amethyst, you have already been married to an older man. You need company of your own age."

"I need you," she said tensely.

"And we could never marry," he reminded her.

"I am not talking of marriage – merely of housekeeping for you, rearing your children – "

"Sleeping in my bed? No, Amethyst! I'll not sleep with you or live in the same house or have you take care of the babes." He spoke firmly, his face implacable. "If you choose to stay in Wales you will have to live at Foster Farm. I will engage a reliable woman to keep house for me, and you must marry again. In a year or two you must take another husband, start a family of your own. You cannot live your life through me."

"You're cruel," she said dully. "I don't know why I love you."

"It is not love. It's a childish fantasy and I'll not indulge you. I am forty years old, Amethyst, and the only woman I ever loved has died. I will never take another wife and, if in time I choose to take a mistress, you will not be she."

His voice was cold ice closing about her heart. She had not fully realised until this moment how much she had counted on his loving her, but there was no affection in his eyes as they rested on her. Somehow, without knowing quite how it had happened, she had begun to lose him.

"Excuse me." She spoke swiftly, rising from her chair. "I feel the need for some air, some time to be by myself. Excuse me."

Walking rapidly across the hall and through the courtyard she found herself on the path that threaded a brown ribbon through the pale wheat. All about the house the rowan trees stood, proud in their scarlet and green. She began to cry, tears blurring her vision, her feet stumbling over a rut. A pair of muscular arms steadied her, closed about her, and she blinked up at Will Bohanna.

"Mistress Amethyst! I heard you were back." His voice held unfeigned pleasure but there was concern in his eyes as he gazed at her.

"Will!" She shook herself free, blinking rapidly. "I arrived yesterday. You know my – my husband died."

"And was sorry to hear it. I had meant to write but I was never much a hand at putting my feelings down on paper."

"Or into words of any kind. I was disappointed that you were not here to greet me."

"I would have been, but Adam's fretful with cutting his back teeth," he explained. "You know I've a son now?"

"Yes. Yes, I heard."

"And Mair is in the family way again. We'd like a girl next time."

"You're happy, then?" She spoke wistfully.

"Happy enough." He stooped to pick up the fowling-piece he had let drop when he held her. "One cannot have full happiness all the time."

"But Mair is a good wife, is she not?"

"Yes." His voice conveyed nothing, but there was yearning in his eyes.

"And a good mother?"

"That too," he said briefly. "But she is not you. She never

could be you, Amethyst. No woman could compare with you."

"Oh, Will, I have been such a fool!" she burst out impulsively, "I thought I wanted more than this place or these people. I allowed Richard Clare to persuade me into marriage and it was the worst bargain I ever made. He was so old and crotchety, Will. He would not let me come home even for a visit, you know. I did not have an opportunity of seeing my poor mother before she died. I shall never see her again and she was always so sweet to me!"

"But you have seen the babes?"

"And love them dearly," she said warmly. "I grew up all alone but they will have one another for company. At least they will have that."

"But you are staying here now, surely?" he said, looking surprised. "You will act as housekeeper for Master Schneider?"

"No! No, I cannot stay here now!" she said, beginning to hurry on. "I had hoped to stay for this is my home. In Chester I felt like a bird in a cage, but I must go back there. I cannot stay here."

"But surely you will … " he began.

"It is impossible!" She stood still, her head bowed, tears glinting on her cheeks. "Oh, Will, I cannot tell you! Don't ask me!"

"But we are friends, are we not? We are still friends?" He caught at her hand, his palm rough against her smooth one.

"Once you hoped for something more," she said brokenly, "and I thrust you away. I've no right now to burden you with my troubles."

"Cannot Master Schneider advise you?"

"Jan? Oh, don't speak to me of him!" she cried. "He is all the cause of my grief! I have offered to keep house for him and rear the children, and he has insulted me grossly. Dear God! I cannot tell you the manner of his insult, but you may imagine it. He said such things – wicked, lewd! My poor mother would have died if she had known the thoughts that ran in his mind! I don't know what to do! I don't know where to turn!"

She was speaking into thin air. Will Bohanna had released her hand and was running towards the house. She opened her mouth to call him back but no sound emerged. She could not remember exactly what she had said, only that her anger was spent. Jan ought to be punished for the manner in which he had rejected her offer of love, she was eaten up with love that nobody wanted!

A shot rang out clearly and a blackbird flew out from one of the rowan trees, scattering berries. Amethyst's own head jerked up her eyes widening to encompass the blue of the arching sky, and then she was running too, tramping wheat stalks, slamming the gate back on its hinges.

"I killed him," Will said blankly as she ran into the parlour. She had no memory of crossing the hall. It was as if she had always stood, looking down at Jan.

"I killed him," Will said again. His face was wiped clean of all expression and the gun dangled limply from his hand. "I don't know how it happened. I didn't mean – he's dead."

"An accident! It was an accident," she gasped out, shaking him. "The gun went off by accident."

"No, it couldn't have done. I pointed it. One never points a gun."

"Save to demonstrate a shot. You were demonstrating a

good shot you'd made and the gun went off. We were all laughing and joking and then the gun went off. I was here and I saw it.''

"The gun went off," he said in a stupid, befuddled way.

"By accident. Will, you have a wife and son and another child on the way. You cannot leave them while you rush off to confess! You must think of your family.''

"I was thinking of you," he said dully. "I am thinking only of you.''

"Think of yourself," she said. "You will be hanged if you tell them the truth, Will. There will be the most terrible scandal! People might even say that you and I were lovers, that you were jealous – ''

"Incest! It would have been incest if he had touched you.''

"We'll not talk of it." She shook him again, fixing him with the intensity of her gaze, her mind working clearly and coldly. "We were here, the three of us, jesting about your markmanship. You raised the gun to demonstrate and it went off. It went off by accident, Will. I can bear witness to that.''

"I don't remember anything," he said. "I was angry and then there was a flash, a report – ''

"Jesting, Will! You were jesting! We were jesting and the gun went off. Take Cariad from the stable and ride for the doctor. Tell him there has been an accident.''

"An accident." He nodded, the shock still blurring his voice. "We were jesting and there was an accident.''

"That's right, Will! Now ride for the doctor. No, leave the gun here. That's right. Ride for the doctor and tell him there's been an accident. An *accident*!'' she gave him a frantic push and he shambled through the door, his limbs moving in an awkward, unrhythmic way, his eyes glazed as if he sleepwalked.

Nobody else could have been close enough to hear the shot. Old Jane, who was practically stone deaf, was having an afternoon nap upstairs with the three children. Surprisingly, none of them had woken up either.

It had happened so quickly that she could not absorb the reality of it. Jan was dead. The man she loved was dead, and all her plans had come to nothing. She was nineteen years old and her hope of happiness was smashed. At the last Jan had escaped her loving. He lay, blood still oozing sluggishly from the wound in his temple, his eyes half open, faint surprise on his face. He was not Jan any longer. He was an empty shell, the substance fled to be with Isobel.

"I have got children," she said aloud. "Lowell and Prester and little Rowan. I have them and they have me." One day she would have 'Rowan Garth' too. One day. She would have that despite every obstacle. Kneeling to close Jan's eyes she began to cry again. Her tears were genuine but her heart was all ice now.